THE
STREET
OF THE
LAUGHING
CAMEL

BEN LUCIEN BURMAN

THE STREET
OF THE

McGRAW-HILL BOOK COMPANY, INC.

LAUGHING
CAMEL

Drawings by ALICE CADDY

NEW YORK   TORONTO   LONDON

THE STREET OF THE LAUGHING CAMEL

FIRST EDITION

For George W. Healy, Jr.

CHAPTER ONE

My name's Yance. Yance Cullum. I come from Black Spring, Texas. That ain't far from San Antonio. Ain't a real town. Just a wide place in the road, the way they say.

It all started in Africa at the end of the war when I was standing by the little river in Algeria and I seen the Arab women washing their clothes by rubbing them with rocks. The river was in a little place named Bab-El-Kebir, what they call a oasis, at the edge of the Sahara.

When I said what I was going to do the captain of my old Army outfit and the other Americans told me I was crazy. They told me Americans in their right mind didn't go fooling around with Arabs that way. They said I'd get killed or something worse.

I guess I am pretty lucky to be still alive. A couple of times it was awful close. It's a funny place, that Africa, full of all kinds of things. There's plenty that happened I ain't figured out yet.

I guess I didn't tell you right about the women rubbing the rocks. It started before that, 'way back when I was a kid ten years old and we were so poor after my father was killed braking trains on the Southern Pacific, and I seen my mother slaving away working as a hired woman for the people in Black Spring so we could have something to eat.

I figured then I was going to get her some money soon as I could so she wouldn't have to work that way. I'd make us like the other Cullums in Texas, big people, owned ranches and are judges and sheriffs and things.

I rode fences for one of them rich Cullums owned a ranch near Victoria. And because we both had the same name, when I left he gave me a picture of himself and wrote his name on it, James C. Cullum. He was sure a fine fellow.

I started helping the cowhands around Black Spring when I was twelve, I guess, and by the time I was sixteen I was rounding up a steer as good as anybody. Ma didn't want me to be a cowboy. Her daddy had a little grocery store out in Illinois and she wanted me to be a clerk for somebody in Black Spring so I could end up having my own business like her father, a grocery or a shoe store or something.

"Nobody ever starved to death that owned a grocery," Ma always used to say. "Working for other people never gets you anywhere."

2

I punched cattle for maybe five years. And I seen I wasn't putting no money in the bank. And then a rodeo happened to come to town and they gave me a job. It was kind of hard on you, busting up your arms and legs and leaving you all black and blue, till you looked like one of them jellyroll slices you get sometimes when you're having a fancy meal at a restaurant. But I was a good rider and made pretty good money.

After a while I had something saved up, and I seen a little grocery a Polack had for sale in San Antonio, and Ma liked it, too, and I bought it.

We was doing fine, and then one day a fellow came from what they call the wholesale house with a couple of policemen. Seems like the Polack hadn't paid for a nickel's worth of the groceries in the place, just took my money and lit out for the prairie. I didn't own a can of tomatoes.

I tried a couple of things after that, driving a cab for a while in San Antonio. And I used to hear them big business men riding in my cab talk the same as Ma, how having your own business was the only way of living. And I sure felt bad about losing that grocery. But I needed money so I got a job at the Ford plant in Houston. Working in the Parts Department. That's where they keep the parts. And then the war come and I joined the Army, and pretty soon I was on my way to Africa.

I was in the fighting around Tunis, and I was off by myself in a kind of gully when I come on one of our boys that was hit by a machine gun. "Get me some water, will you, buddy?" he says.

Well, when a man or a cow wants water you find it. The Germans were shooting around pretty fancy, but I saw a spring a little way off and started crawling over. I got hit

3

on the way, but it didn't feel like much, and I filled up my canteen and come back. I gave the fellow the drink and then I saw he's pretty sick so I pick him up and carry him back to the lines and they fix him up all right.

And then they see I'm kind of shot up, too, and they put me in the hospital and work on me for a few months. And then they sent me off to the big rest camp at Bab-El-Kebir and that's how I seen the women rubbing the rocks.

I was discharged from the rest camp, but I got stuck there with a replacement outfit till the war ended, and I had to figure out what I was going to do. The country around Bab-El-Kebir was desert land, kind of the way it is in Texas. And if you're a desert fellow like me, I guess there ain't nothing else for you. When you see them yellow mountains with a eagle over the top, shining like the eagle on a new silver dollar, it sure makes you want to write a poem about it.

I wrote a couple of poems when I was a cowboy. One was about a cowboy and his horse, and the other was about the American flag.

I wrote a poem once, too, when I was driving a cab. It was about a mother and her baby I drove to the hospital one afternoon. I saw she was terrible poor, and when she looked at the meter it was $2.75, and I saw her face, and I told her not to pay no attention to the meter, and I gave her a five-dollar bill. And driving back I thought out the poem, kind of imagining what happened to her in the hospital. How her husband was in bed and couldn't move, and how glad he was to see her and the baby and things like that. I was going with a girl that worked in the Wagon Diner, where the cabdrivers ate, and I showed the poem to her and she said it was nice.

Well, some of the fellows around Bab-El-Kebir began talking about staying in Africa, maybe going to South Africa and Johannesburg or maybe down at the rubber plantations in Liberia. Africa was so big and so many kinds of things were sure to be turning up, everybody figured it'd be a fine place to make money. So I began thinking maybe I'd stay too.

I had all my back pay and I was figuring maybe I'd buy some little business in Algiers or Casablanca or somewheres, maybe a little grocery again or a radio or auto repair shop, and then when I'd made a little money, send over for Ma. She wasn't doing so good in Houston now. She was kind of lonesome and sick with the asthma.

I'd have liked to stay in Bab-El-Kebir, because it was the desert, the way I said, and it'd be special good for the asthma. But it was a little place and I couldn't see no way of making a living.

I guess what really fixed it was the fellow from the Moose. Before coming to Africa we was at a camp in New Jersey, and the Moose Lodge from Jersey City gave us a party one night in the clubhouse. And I met a fellow there owned a laundry, and I got to talking to him about the business I thought of going into when I got out of the Army, and he told me what a fine business laundrying was, no matter what happened, hard times or anything.

"What you got to do first when you're starting a business is to find out what people need," he said. "And people are always needing clean clothes."

I knew he was sure right. I remembered how Ma looked when she was slaving over the tub, all wore out, washing the cowboys' clothes at Black Spring to make a extra dollar.

Funny how things are, ain't it? I guess it was maybe four years after I talked to the fellow at the Moose, and I'm in Algiers on leave for a few days from Bab-El-Kebir, trying to figure out whether to go back to the States or stay. And I'm walking down a side street when we pass a little laundry with a sign in the window saying it was for sale.

And all of a sudden what the Moose fellow said and seeing Ma leaning over the washtub and the women rubbing the rocks in the little river all run together, and I knew what I wanted to do.

I'd have my own business the way Ma and the big fellows that rode in my cab were always talking about. And with Africa booming the way it was, it'd be a business that was sure to be a big success. Because, like the Moose fellow told me, it was something the people needed bad.

I'd start a laundry over here in Africa.

But I wouldn't put it in a big place like Algiers. I'd start it where they needed it most, in Bab-El-Kebir where there were all those Arabs had to get their washing done, and the closest laundry was three hundred miles away.

So I went in and told the little Frenchman that owned the place I'd buy it.

My old company commander was in Algiers and, like I told you, he thought I was crazy.

"Take it easy, Cullum," he said. "You're going to get yourself into awful trouble. Go gold mining or hunting uranium if you want to. But don't start a thing like a laundry where you'll get all mixed up with the Arab religion and end up with a dagger in your liver."

The others all said the same thing. But I didn't answer. I figure you got to go your own way the best you can, no matter what anybody tells you. I read in a book once people did plenty of arguing with Thomas A. Edison.

CHAPTER TWO

WELL, IN A COUPLE OF WEEKS they gave me my discharge in Algiers, and I picked up a surplus Army jeep and a little trailer to hook onto it for pretty near nothing, and then I went over to pick up the laundry machinery from the Frenchman.

There were washtubs and wringers, and what they call a mangle, that's a kind of big ironer for sheets and things run by electricity, and a big electric washing machine some Arab women had put rocks in before the Frenchman told them how it worked and now it didn't do so good.

And I piled them all into the trailer, and before you know it I'm rolling on my way to Bab-El-Kebir.

7

The road I took ran straight across what they call the Atlas Mountains, and it was sure a trip. You'd be going around a narrow place on a cliff so steep it seemed like the eagles you passed were five miles below you, when all of a sudden a bunch of camels would come towards you each loaded with a tree that stuck way out over the road, and no sign of a driver anywhere.

And you'd have to get out, and coax each camel to squeeze against the wall, at the same time you were driving the trailer past on two wheels pretty near.

I got across the mountains at last and then I saw Bab-El-Kebir spread out in the flat country down below me. It looked like it was made of gold. I bet if one of them Spanish explorers I used to hear about in Texas come there searching for the gold cities of the Indians they'd have figured they didn't need to go any farther. Course, when you got there it wasn't really gold. It was just the houses made of yellow stone and adobe shining in the sun.

I rode into the town, and I could see the little river running right through the middle with gardens and rows of date palms along each side, just like the picture on the packages of dates I used to buy in the Wagon Diner when I was driving a cab and couldn't stop to eat. When I was eating them dates I sure never figured I'd be right there in the picture. Up above was a little hill where the French Army had a fort, and some Frenchmen on horses come out the gate blowing horns, and then back of them rode some Arab soldiers they called Spahis, carrying big swords and wearing red capes.

Right outside the town were big sand dunes, stretching so far it looked like there was enough sand to make a bathing beach around the world fifty times. People said it was

8

the beginning of the Sahara. Some of the dunes had Bedouins on them—that's what they call the Arabs live in the desert—and you could see their tents, all striped like a barber pole, only the stripes were black. In the tents you could hear flutes playing and drums beating for somebody that was dancing.

People are sure different, ain't they? Back home in Black Spring when you didn't have nothing special to do you ate a piece of pie in a restaurant or went to a movie. In Bab-El-Kebir you danced and played the flute.

I drove through the town, full of camels and goats and all kinds of funny-dressed Arabs and women wearing veils. And then all the Arab kids come out like mice from the little doorways and began running beside the car, hollering and yelling and asking for pennies.

I got to the French hotel where I was going to stay and the next day rented a little store from a old Arab with a white beard made him look like them pictures of Moses in the Bible. The building was made of yellow stone like the other houses, with a little window and a counter and a couple of rooms in back. It was on the main street, right in front of the big tourist hotel where all the rich people stayed, and I figured it'd be a good place. The name of the street was The Street of the Laughing Camel.

I put a army cot in the little room right back of the store with a table and a couple of them Arab cushions so I'd have a place to sleep and eat. And then in the bigger room back of that I started fixing up the mangle and the washer and things so we could do the laundry work there.

I was standing out in front one day, resting a minute, when I hear somebody behind me say, "Okay, Joe."

I turned around quick, expecting to see somebody out

9

of my old outfit, but it ain't a American at all. It's a Arab, a skinny little fellow wearing a red hat and a red coat and red pants with a blue stripe on them that you could see right away was the uniform of one of them kind of French soldiers they call Zouaves, that he'd got hold of someway and cut down to fit.

He's young, about the same age as me maybe, but he's awful small, like a jockey, with a funny drawed-up face. With that red Arab hat and the red uniform, he looked just like a organ-grinder monkey a Italian had around Black Spring for a while, especially when the monkey was asking you to give him a penny. When he talked you almost expected him to give a monkey squeak.

"You and me's buddies, Joe," he said. He had a funny way of speaking I couldn't figure out. It was all mixed up, half a kind of fancy English and half a kind that you could tell he picked up from the soldiers at the rest camp.

"I give you a present, Joe," he told me. "Won't cost you nothing. Just because you and me buddies. Okay?"

He held out a Arab cane all carved up and painted like a rainbow. You saw plenty of those canes around Bab-El-Kebir. You couldn't walk a hundred feet down the road without a Arab wanting to give you one for a present. And if you took it, before you were through he had every nickel on you.

Course I didn't take the cane.

The Arab kept on talking. "You need to buy something, Joe?" he says. "Perfume? Whisky? Penicillin maybe make you sick? I save you plenty money."

I told him I didn't need nothing.

"You need somebody to work for you, Joe? I'm good

10

man. Sweep out for you. Cook your cous-cous. Okay?"

"Ever work for an American or a Frenchman?" I said, because I'd been figuring I'd need somebody to talk Arab when I got things going.

"Sure, sure, Joe," he answered, smiling a kind of monkey smile, all excited. "I work last summer two months for the Frenchman that is the Chief of Police. When I am in the jail for picking a pocket."

I was just going to tell him I didn't think I'd want nobody after all when a bunch of beggars came up, each one carrying a bowl and holding out his hand for money. I gave each one some change, but the big fellow all wrapped in burlap that was in front showed me they wanted more. I gave them more money, and the big fellow made signs again that it wasn't near enough.

I didn't know what to do with them fellows all pulling at me, and I was looking around kind of desperate, like in a rodeo when you've got a bad steer and you can't throw him down and the crowd's all hollering against you, when all of a sudden this little fellow that wants a job yells at them Arabs like a wild man, and sends them flying down the street.

A minute later he turns to me. "Look, Joe. You need me plenty, Joe." Like I said, he talked all mixed up. "These city Arabs are terrible thieves. You never heard of such thieves in your country. They will take the bone out of your arm and you will not know it is gone until you try to hold something and your arm folds up like it is rubber. You give me this job, Joe. And I will see nobody cheats you. Not one penny. And I will not cheat you very much. You ask Miss Peckham."

11

"Who's Miss Peckham?" I said.

"She is the Christian missionary here. It is Miss Peckham that has taught me English," he says, and his face lights up like the sun shining on the fancy gold doorway of the tourist hotel across the street. "She comes from Fall River in Massachusetts. Miss Peckham's church in Fall River sends me fine presents every Christmas and on my birthday. Miss Peckham says I am like a son to her. She has been here thirty years. I am her only convert."

Well, I knew I sure needed somebody, so I figured I'd better give him the job. He said his name was Mohammed Ben Tahib or something. But course you couldn't call nobody by a name like that. So I done what us fellows in the Army always done with people wherever we was, whether they was Arabs or Italians or Frenchmen, just called them Mac or Doc maybe. So I called this here fellow Louie.

With Louie helping me things got ready fast, and I started to figure about hiring people to do the laundry. The Frenchman in Algiers told me two girls would be enough, and I asked Louie if he had a couple of sisters maybe, because I'd like to get somebody I knew about. The fellow at the Moose had told me the big thing you got to watch in a laundry is stealing the clothes.

Louie looked at me kind of funny. "Sure, sure, Joe," he said after a minute. "I got plenty sisters."

He goes off and comes back in an hour with a big fat Arab woman wearing a veil and all wrapped up in layers of sheets like when you wrap up a glass bowl so it won't break in the mail.

"This is my sister, Joe," he says, but when she takes off her veil inside the store I couldn't see no kind of resemblance.

12

Then he goes off again and comes back this time with a Arab woman so old she wasn't wearing a veil at all, with her skin wrinkled like one of those dry river beds they have in Texas, and with kind of slant eyes and a Chinese face like some of them Bedouin tribes you seen around there that you'd swear come straight from Shanghai. She looked old enough to be the fat woman's mother.

She's kind of holding back, but Louie pushes her forward. "This is another sister, Joe," he said.

I hired them and got ready for the opening.

It was interesting watching all the things out in front that went along The Street of the Laughing Camel. There were lemonade sellers rattling little brass cups, and Arab policemen in shiny uniforms, and donkeys so loaded down with hay you couldn't see anything but the hoofs of their four legs, and French soldiers smoking cigarettes, and camels with Bedouin women sitting on them like a circus parade, and sheep and goats running everywhere with a man behind yelling at them and trying to hold them in with a stick, and once in a while a Arab on a white horse, looking like a sultan.

I always liked learning about queer kinds of places. When I was in the Parts Department they had what they called a social meeting every month for improving your mind, the way they say. And they'd always have a speaker came from some place 'way off, maybe the Ford plant in Japan or India or somewhere.

I went every time. Like I told you, I ain't had no education much. I had to stop school in the fifth grade. And when you're that way you got to do the best you can. The meetings was generally the first Tuesday in the month, but after a while they changed it to Wednesday. They gave you cream-cheese-and-peanut-butter sandwiches and coffee free. You could get beer if you wanted but you had to pay for that. It was ten cents a bottle.

Me and Louie worked late at night, finishing things up. The gasoline torches where the date sellers were sitting would go out one after the other and everybody would be asleep. And the oasis would be quiet as a graveyard. Even the moonlight was different here. The moon was so bright when it was shining they turned out the electric lamps in the street. You could even see the colors in the mountains, yellow, and red, and purple, just like the paintbox you had in school.

And sometimes after Louie would go home I'd sit listening to the sounds in the desert and think about riding the range and Ma and the cab driving and everything and wonder how I'd come to such a queer place and what was going to happen to me.

Like I said, I wasn't worried about getting killed or anything, the way the company commander had been talking. Course, I knew there were bandits out in the hills that came into town once in a while and would murder you for a coughdrop. Every Arab house had walls around it like a fort and locks so big and strong you almost had to hire somebody to help you carry the key.

A couple of times I woke up in the night and thought I heard something prowling around outside. But I figured it was a goat or a hyena maybe, so I didn't pay any attention. There was a couple of Italians had a store there, and one of them had been knifed awful bad just the day after I came, but I figured that was because he'd been going around with Arab women. And course anything about their women with the Arabs was a terrible thing.

But I was worried about the laundry. Because I sure wanted it to be a success. It wasn't only the money so I could bring Ma over and make her happy. Like I told you, I'd been wanting a little business for a long while. It's just nice that way, having something to think about every day and watching it kind of grow a little at a time, and always trying to make it better. I guess it's like having a kid maybe.

And I wanted it to go because I thought it'd be a nice thing for the people in the town, too. One night, maybe a week after we landed in Africa, what they call a U.S. Consul come out to the camp to give a talk about the Arabs in the hall where they had the USO shows, and I went to hear it.

This fellow wasn't near as good as the people that come to the socials of the Parts Department. He was kind of stuck up and talked kind of stiff. But he said something that ain't left my mind since.

He said we was strangers here in a strange land and that each of us was what they call a U.S. Ambassador. He said it was our duty to show the Arabs that Americans was nice people and the way Americans do things. He said we was never to forget that wherever we went, in a church or a dance hall or a bar, that it was as if each of us was carrying a American flag.

It was just as if we was the President.

I guess I'm built kind of funny. A idea like that'll get to rolling and rolling around in my head, and it won't roll out easy.

Well, about the time I had everything ready in Bab-El-Kebir, a fellow that had been a sergeant in the tank corps came through on his way down in the desert to work for a company that was looking for oil, and him and me got to talking about the laundry.

You could see right away he was a awful smart fellow. He said before he went into the Army he'd been working a couple of years in a supermarket in California, and he said the way it looked to him what I ought to do was get the laundry started off with a real opening like they done with this supermarket in California. He said to fix the place up pretty with flowers, and give everybody that came hot dogs and hamburgers, and maybe calendars or something for souvenirs.

And I got to thinking and it sure sounded the way I'd heard them big business people talking in my cab in San Antonio. I figured he sure was right and decided to do what he said.

So the day before the laundry was ready to open, I go with Louie down to the end of The Street of the Laughing Camel where there's some Arabs broiling meat on kind of icepicks over a charcoal fire. And we show them how to make hot dogs and hamburgers, like the sergeant told us, and ask them to get a lot ready for tomorrow. Louie had eat hot dogs and hamburgers a couple of times when the soldiers gave him some at the rest camp.

When I really got to thinking I wasn't worried about the opening too much. It wasn't as if I hadn't had no business experience. Because course I'd had the grocery I bought from the Polack.

The next morning the sun was shining bright and pretty like it done every day, and Louie comes in, all dressed up in a new red hat and a red what they call a burnoose I'd give him the money for, that's a kind of robe like them old Romans wore I seen in the movies. He'd brought some flowers and put them around the counter and everywhere and the place looked real nice. And then the two Arab women came, the fat one and the old one, and they had new kind of robes I'd give them, too, white and shiny as a floor in a bank.

I guess everybody had been talking about the laundry, because when the two women come there were already some people out in front waiting. And in a little while all kinds of Arabs were standing in line just like for a movie back home.

There were Arab porters with nothing but a piece of burlap around their waists, big-chested fellows carrying a whole wardrobe maybe or a bale of alfalfa on their heads. There were date sellers, looking like them little plaster Chinamen with fat stomachs you buy at carnivals for good luck. There were Bedouin women with rugs they'd brought in town to sell, and Bedouin men with their camels, and the camels were grunting and groaning all the time something awful.

And course there were all kinds of beggars; blind beggars that really couldn't see and beggars just pretending; beggar women holding babies weren't no more than six months old and still they'd smile at you and put out a hand for money; and religious beggars that stood like statues, looking down on everybody, not asking for anything, just saying words from what they call the Koran.

Seemed like everybody in Bab-El-Kebir was there and more besides.

"Looks to me like we're starting off wonderful," I said to Louie.

The Arab meat men came in pretty soon with the frankfurters and the hamburgers, and I piled them up on a table near the counter, and the Arabs put their charcoal stoves right by. And then I put some big baskets behind the counter where the two women could put the bundles of laundry people brought. And I looked around to see if everything was all right and opened the door. The Arabs rushed in so fast you could pretty near hear them whistle, and they dived onto them hamburgers and franks like cats I seen once when a meat truck fell over on Highway 81 just outside of San Antonio. In about a minute all them eats was gone.

I sent out for more right away, and when they was finished sent out for new ones. I sent out maybe twenty times, I guess. And then like the sergeant said, I gave them each a souvenir, one of them little puzzles you seen where you roll little white balls under a glass until they drop into the mouth of a clown or a bear and make the teeth. I'd bought them from a Syrian fellow I met when I was in Algiers and he said his brother'd been traveling down in the desert all his life and the Arabs was crazy about puzzles.

He said his brother was going to sell them to a big Frenchman for a lot of money, because they were hard to get, but he figured since I was his friend and just starting out and the puzzles'd help me so much, he'd make his brother sell them to me instead for half price.

The Arabs sure liked them, the way he said. It was nice to watch them eating the hot dogs and shaking the puzzles at the same time.

It got toward sunset and what they call the muezzin in the mosque tower called out the way he did every day for evening prayer, and the last Arab went out the door. I hadn't had no time to think about the laundry people had brought and things like that till now. And I went behind the counter where I'd put the baskets to hold the bundles of clothes to be washed. I figured with all this crowd that the Arabs would have brought plenty.

And I looked in the baskets and I felt all paralyzed, the way I did the afternoon I was rounding up strays and my horse threw me when it went down in a gopher hole and I lay out by myself not able to move for almost a day, thinking my back was broke.

There wasn't a single bundle.

The Arabs had just come for the hamburgers and the souvenirs.

CHAPTER THREE

I WAS STANDING THERE by the counter feeling terrible, with Louie looking black as the bottom of a coal mine I was in once, when all of a sudden I see him rush out the door.

He came back pretty soon with a little old lady wearing the kind of clothes I seen in the books the women used to wear thirty or forty years ago, a little black hat and a black dress so stiff when she walked you could almost hear it crack.

There was a little old lady in Black Spring dressed that

way when I was a kid. She was a music teacher, went around giving piano lessons to the girls, and she played the organ in the Baptist church. When she died the Baptists gave her a wonderful funeral. They sent all the way to Houston for the preacher, and they said he sure was worth the train fare. The music teacher looked just like this old lady in Bab-El-Kebir.

There were two Arab boys walking in front of her, one of them with a big pile of blankets on his head, and the other carrying a basket that I could see was filled up with sheets and towels and things.

Louie was grinning the way a organ-grinder monkey would do if you gave him half a dollar.

"It's Miss Peckham," he said. "She's brought the Mission cleaning and laundry."

I put out my hand and she took it almost like she was scared, as if she was afraid of shaking hands with a man maybe. She sure reminded me of that little music teacher in Black Spring. Her skin was like fine writing paper, the kind somebody gave you for a present when you were a kid and you kept it in the box afraid to use it till it got old, with tiny lines running through everywhere. And she had a awful sweet look in her face, you know, one of them old ladies that never did a bad thing or seen a bad thing in their lives, just go around helping sick people and doing good things like that every minute. The preacher at the funeral in Black Spring for the music teacher said she was a saint, and you was sure when this old lady in Bab-El-Kebir died, the preacher would get up and say she was a saint the same way.

She looked at me so long without talking I got kind of embarrassed.

"I speak English so little I have almost forgotten," she said, like she was apologizing. Her voice was awful shaky and she talked kind of stiff, like them New England people I seen when a buddy of mine drove a truckload of fancy cattle up to the place of a rich fellow near Boston and I went along. "Mohammed here—he tells me you call him Louis—is the only one to whom I can speak in English. I do not know what I would do without Mohammed. He is my only convert. I am proud of Mohammed. He is a good Christian."

She straightened out the blankets the boy had dropped on the counter and made a neat pile. "I also have the Fall River paper every day, except of course on Sundays. I have had it sent ever since the Lord called me here thirty years ago. It makes me seem close to my friends and keeps me from being lonely."

She looked kind of worried for a minute. "Are you an atheist? I hear so many in America today are atheists. I would be distressed to have my blankets cleaned by an atheist."

"My people in Texas was all Methodists," I said. "And I had a uncle out in Oklahoma was a Holy Roller preacher."

She went on talking like she didn't hear. I guess she hadn't been around anybody from home that she could speak to for so long it was like she was talking to herself.

"I prefer Moslems to atheists," she said. "Though they have sometimes made my life a grievous trial."

Her face got kind of sad, like once I seen the music teacher's when she was passing the saloon in Black Spring and a couple of drunk cowboys were coming out. "I do not wish to complain. I do not question the ways of the Lord. But the souls of the Arabs are like iron. I am seventy-six years of age. I have not too long to live. If only the Lord would grant me another convert before I die, I would be happy. . . . Would you care to come to the Mission Church some Sunday? We have Sunday School at nine and full divine service at eleven. Perhaps you will come four Sundays from now, that will be the first Sunday in May. It will be just eight years ago that day that my son Mohammed here became my convert. We celebrate it every year as a beautiful anniversary."

She hurried out the door.

Well, it sure made me feel good to see Miss Peckham, even if she was a missionary, and I ain't ever been much of a fellow for going to church. Except for the sergeant that worked in the supermarket, I hadn't seen no Americans for a while, because the rest camp was all closed up. I guess I was getting pretty lonesome.

But the laundry she brought wasn't no help; it didn't keep us busy any time. And when it was done, the girls just stood around talking and listening to the music I played on the radio. There still wasn't a single Arab that came with a bundle. I didn't know why. I figured maybe it was against their religion or something.

A couple of days after the opening the police chief walked over to see me, a big red-faced Frenchman named Dumont, with what they call handle-bar mustaches, to find out whether I was a spy, I guess. He was a good-natured kind of fellow, always smoking a pipe with clouds of smoke around him so thick you could hardly see his mustaches, and that French tobacco was so strong just being in a room with him a minute'd pretty near choke you to death. Him and me got to be good friends, though, and he give me some shirts to wash.

A few times some Americans come from the big hotel across the street, because they saw the sign *New York Laundry* I hung outside like the sergeant from the supermarket told me. He said New York was a good name to get customers. I guess the Americans wanted to see somebody from home, the same as me. They'd bring me a few socks or T-shirts, or maybe a little dry cleaning. But I knew if something didn't happen soon the laundry'd have to close up.

Louie was as worried as me. We was mighty good friends now and I guess plenty of times if it hadn't been for him I'd have started back to America.

He was a funny little fellow. Sometimes he'd look awful tricky, like the organ-grinder monkey when he was stealing something out of your pocket. And then when I was awful blue, he'd try to cheer me up, and tell me funny stories about the jails he'd been in and the tricks he'd played on the rich Arabs. Like the time I seen the organ-grinder Italian sitting in front of a store, all wore out, with no money, I guess, and the monkey was on his shoulder, patting the Italian's cheek, and you could tell he was trying to make the Italian feel better.

But Louie couldn't help the laundry business, either.

What made things worse, when I bought the laundry I'd written Ma and told her it looked like I could send over for her quick. And I got a letter back saying her asthma was getting worse. She'd seen somewhere in the paper, she said, that the climate in North Africa, Egypt and Algeria and them places was the best in the world for the asthma,

24

and she was ready to come any minute. Now it looked like I'd have to tell her she couldn't come at all.

I'd sit outside under the awning I'd put up and watch the people go by, specially the ones that come out of the big hotel, and I'd look at their clothes and try to figure out how much laundry they used each week, and how much money I'd get if they brought it to me. Funny, ain't it, how people always look at the things they're interested in. A shoemaker looks at people's shoes, and a barber looks to see how their hair is cut, and a dentist looks at their teeth to see if they need any filling.

I guess I done the laundry in my head that way of everybody in Bab-El-Kebir. I watched the Americans in the hotel special. I guess Americans use more laundry than anybody. Except maybe an Englishman. I stayed at a boarding house in Houston a while and there was a Englishman who was living there. And he used to drive the landlady crazy all the time wanting more soap and towels.

Well, the sergeant that worked in the supermarket said he used to talk to the manager sometimes. And the manager was always telling him the ret of making a big

vas plenty of ich the hey were always hav-
kind of e money. way automobiles and
so tight you I'd drove around in
n were stand-
e opening. zes like they did. But
th all of them drugstore near me had
aiting to jump glass jar full of beans
't believe my to the fellow guessing
the jar.
e written on at couldn't do no harm
at looks like and filled it with beans

and put it in the window like they did at the drugstore, and Louie printed a notice in Arab saying that anybody that came inside, whether they brought any laundry or not, would have a chance to guess free.

It started out better than I figured and a lot of Arabs come. I gave them each a little ticket I'd made out of cardboard folded in two, and they wrote their names and the number of beans they guessed on both halves, and put one half in the big box I had on the counter for the drawing, and kept the other to show in case they won. The first prize was three dollars, the second was two dollars, and there was two what they call booby prizes of a dollar each one.

Course the Arabs didn't bring any laundry, but it looked busy anyhow. And the way the sergeant said the manager told him, if you kept them coming long enough, pretty soon they'd be customers and be bringing clothes. Most of them couldn't write, so they'd have a friend along to fix up the tickets.

Saturday morning came, the day that was the end of the contest, and I counted the beans and put down the number on a piece of paper. And right after lu
Arabs started walking in to see who'd won th
There was a lot of them, packing the store
couldn't breathe hardly, and plenty of the
ing outside, too. It was almost as bad as th

I go up to the box and pull out a ticket, w
watching me like a fox does a chicken he's w
on, and I look at the number, and I can
eyes. It said 2381, just exactly the number in

I told Louie to read out the Arab's nam
the bottom. And a porter with long hair t

Samson in the Bible comes up grinning, and I give him the three dollars.

I take out another stub. And this time I think I'm going crazy. It has the same 2381 again, just like the first.

I couldn't figure it out. I hadn't told nobody, Louie or the women either. I thought maybe it was some of that Arab mind reading you see in them vaudeville shows, where they tell you the number of a dollar bill you're holding or the initials of your girl.

I asked Louie to read out the name of the second stub, and when I paid that fellow, I pulled out the third. It wasn't no different, either.

I reached in the tin box and pulled out a whole handful. Every one of them is 2381.

I was standing there, trying to think whether I ought to pay the two third prizes, when all of a sudden them Arabs just kind of exploded, like the time I seen a sewer blow up in San Antonio when somebody throwed in a match and it was full of gas. They was all on top of me, shaking their tickets and yelling and hollering like lions and trying to tear the money away from the two fellows that had it already.

I don't know what they'd have done if somebody out on the street hadn't heard all the noise and called the police. And the chief, Mr. Dumont, came with a couple of Arabs and got them all out in a hurry.

They'd mussed things up a lot and broke the window, and I was feeling pretty bad. And then all of a sudden Louie, who'd been watching me kind of funny, dropped to his knees in front of me and tears began running down his little monkey face like a dry river in Texas when it starts flooding after a heavy rain.

"Kill me, Joe," he sobbed. "It's me, Louie, that's done this terrible thing to you."

"You mean you gave them the numbers?" I said.

He started to cry harder. "I counted the beans the first night you put them in the jar, Joe. And then I sold the number to each Arab for three francs. That is a penny in your money. There were two hundred and seventy francs."

He threw a lot of little bills and coins on the floor. "There it is, Joe. Every penny. Take the money, Joe. And then take me to Monsieur Dumont and the jail and tell him to make me crack the rocks again on the road for the rest of my life."

I told him I'd use what he gave me to help pay for the broken window.

He stopped crying and picked up the money from the floor and put it in a pile on the counter. He kind of hesitated, then tears big as marbles started rolling down his cheeks again.

He jerked out a lot more little bills and coins and threw them with the others. "There is another two hundred and seventy francs I was keeping, Joe. I charged them each six francs, not three, for the number."

Course I didn't do anything. I couldn't get nowhere now without Louie. Besides, you got to take people the way they come. If you catch a baby coyote, no matter how you train him, when the moon comes out he's going to run around in a circle and howl like a coyote just the same.

You learn that fast when you're a cowboy.

CHAPTER FOUR

The weather was getting hot now and everybody began sleeping on the roofs. Inside the houses even when the sun set it was just like the time in Houston I was out at the steel mill and stood in front of the door of one of them big furnaces. The heat almost knocked you down.

It was nice laying outside looking up at the stars and listening to the sounds all around you, some Arab girl 'way off singing a love song, and the drums beating and the hyenas out in the desert kind of coughing, and the camels grunting and a donkey braying like he'd waked up out of a bad dream.

And then you'd look down underneath you in the street and see a Arab policeman walking past or maybe six blind holy men that always went around together, chanting to themselves and holding out their bowls for pennies, though except for the policeman there wasn't even a dog anywhere. Or sometimes there'd be a redheaded holy man carrying a incense burner that he'd wave around you for good luck.

And then you'd think there was a big fire in the sky, and it'd be the moon coming up, and you'd see all the other people on the roofs near you, looking like gold statues. And the policeman in the street and the holy men would be all gold, too.

It was getting on toward the fourth Sunday Miss Peckham talked about that was Louie's anniversary, and she asked me a couple of times to come over to the Mission that special Sunday. She came to the laundry every week now and every time I saw her I sure thought about the music teacher and Black Spring. And there was something that reminded me of Ma, too. I don't know exactly. Maybe it was the sad look Miss Peckham'd get when she was talking about the Arabs, the same kind of look Ma had when I was coming down sick and she didn't have the money to send for a doctor.

Like I told you, I never was much for churchgoing. But I couldn't see where it'd hurt nothing to go to Miss Peckham's church once. So I got up early that morning and when Louie came for me I put on my best suit and went.

I tell you I been around, cowboying and cab driving and being in the Army, and I seen a lot, but I never seen a church service like that. It was so pitiful it pretty near made you cry. Wasn't nothing wrong with the church. It was off in a quiet part of the oasis where there was a lot of big palms and Arab gardens, and was just like one of

30

them little churches with a kind of silver steeple I seen in New England when I went up with my buddy in the truck.

Miss Peckham was waiting for us outside, sitting by a fountain where some birds were drinking. She was wearing her black dress like she always done, and her face was all shining, like the steeple where it was hit by the sun. It looked like she'd been praying.

"We will begin with the Sunday School lesson," she said, and took us to the back of the building where there was a big place just like the Sunday School rooms back in the States. There was a little platform up in front where somebody could stand and rows of benches, I guess maybe enough for a couple of hundred people. But every bench was empty. I kept expecting to see people walking in and sitting down. But not a soul came through the door.

It was neat as a pin and Miss Peckham showed me around, looking terribly proud.

"It is a beautiful Sunday School," she said. "The church and the Sunday School were given to us by the kind people of Fall River when I started the Lord's work."

She started taking me around the rows of seats and stopped in front of some small benches where there's places for forty little kids maybe.

"This is the Infants' Section," she said, and then moved over to where the chairs were regular size. "This is the Junior Class. And there next to it is the Senior. Beyond it is the class for Adults. We have, in all, four classes. When we expand I will have another group between the Senior and the Adults that I will call the Young Adults. But for the present this is not necessary."

She walked along the benches, pointing each one out to me.

"I have named each bench for a person in Fall River who has contributed to the Mission," she said. "And I have painted them all different colors. Perhaps there are some in Fall River who would not hold with me in this matter. But I think that God wishes his Sunday Schools to be gay. After all, God likes color. He has made the rainbow. . . . This pink bench is named Agatha Butterfield. You see the name lettered on the arm. This blue bench is Jessica Adams. This orange bench is my brother, Edgar Peckham. He is a lawyer in Fall River, and he has been most generous. I like to have these benches named for my friends and my family. It makes them seem very near."

She looked at her watch. "It is nine o'clock. It is time to begin classes. I always like to start on time for I think promptness is a virtue we should impress on the Arabs, they are so unaware of time. . . . Mohammed, will you please take your usual place there with Edgar. And perhaps Mr. Cullum will sit beside you, with Jessica Adams."

She rang a bell like the old-fashioned kind the teacher used to have when I was going to school out in Black Spring.

She turned to Louie, sitting next to us. "Mohammed, will you please lead us in the Lord's Prayer."

Louie kind of squirmed and began mumbling under his breath.

He finished and Miss Peckham picked up one of the hymnbooks that were in pockets behind the benches. She walked over to a little organ in a corner.

"We will now sing Number Sixty-two," she said.

She played the organ and when she got through stood in front of me and Louie.

Her face was all shiny again and her voice was all shaky. "I will talk to you this morning of the sheep which was lost and then found. If you cannot hear, will you please tell me and I will come closer. I am afraid my voice is weak with happiness."

She talked for a while, just like the place was full of people, then played another hymn and stood up again.

"This will be the end of the Sunday School class for today," she said. "Mohammed will say the benediction. Then we will go into the church for Divine Services."

She waited till Louie stood up and mumbled something under his breath again, then took us into the church. It was like the churches you see in the movies, with a kind of soft light coming through the windows. The pews were all polished up like a looking glass, but it was just the same as the Sunday School. There wasn't a soul sitting in them anywhere.

You could tell nobody ever came in because one of them big rock snakes that live out in the desert was wriggling down the aisle chasing after a toad that lived in the church maybe. I guess maybe Miss Peckham had left the door open. And some kind of gray-and-yellow-feathered birds were flying around over our heads.

Miss Peckham looked at the snake kind of worried till Louie drove it away.

"I cannot like the snakes, even though I know they are of God's creatures and I should be happy that one of them wishes to come into His church," she said. "The birds brighten my spirit like a sunrise. They make me think of Spring at home in the Berkshire Hills."

She climbed up in the pulpit and opened a big Bible.

"My text for today will be Psalm Ninety-six, verse eleven, 'Let the Heavens rejoice and let the Earth be glad.' For this is a joyful day."

We stayed there a hour while she preached a sermon, just about the way my uncle would have done out in Oklahoma, only quieter. All the time the birds were flying over the pulpit, and once the snake came back and went down the aisle, looking for the toad again.

She finished and we went over to her house next to the church, a Arab house made of stone but fixed up like the kind I seen in New England when I was there with the truck. And she gave us a dinner like the one we had when we stayed the night with the fellow that worked for the man we were taking the cattle to, turkey and squash and pumpkin pie and sweet cider to drink.

I don't know how she got them things in Africa. I guess the church people sent them over.

She stopped in the middle of serving Louie some turkey, and her hands shook a little.

"Sometimes I feel very lonely and sad," she told us. "Sometimes I feel that I could argue with God, and ask Him to make the souls of the Arabs less stubborn. But then I remember Mohammed here and how he came to me. And I know that he is God's symbol I have not lived in vain."

I went home after that and it came into my head me and Miss Peckham were kind of the same. She was trying to get souls, the way they say, and I was trying to get laundry.

It looked like we couldn't do either one.

CHAPTER FIVE

WELL, BUSINESS WAS GETTING worse and worse. I was running short of money, and it looked like I was going to have to give up the laundry sure.

A Army buddy from my outfit that was stationed in Algiers come through, and I was telling him about it.

"You're crazy as a red bug, Yance," he said. "Like the C.O. told you. What you getting out of it? You've thrown away all your back pay. And your life ain't worth a dime fooling around by yourself with these wild Arabs. You know how they been knocking off Americans in the

Kasbah in Algiers every night. One of the fellows they pretty near killed just because the poor guy was cross-eyed and they thought he was looking at a Arab girl. Before you get through it's in the cards you'll get tangled up in something. And one morning you'll wake up and wonder why you can't get out of bed and it'll be because a big knife's got your ribs nailed to the mattress."

But I don't quit that easy.

And then one day, just when it looked like things couldn't go on any more, a Arab with a black beard and wearing a purple what they call a turban come to see me and said he'd heard I needed money, and he said not to let that worry me at all. He said he knowed Americans was fine people and I could have all the money I wanted.

And I just signed a little paper, and he gave me two hundred dollars, and said if I wanted more just to send word to him and he'd come right over. He was sure nice.

After that some of the French and English people living in the oasis brought me part of their washing, but there were just a few of them, so it didn't help much. There was a kind of public bath in town, a pretty place made of stone like the old Roman baths that I seen in the movies, where the Emperors and the rich Roman fellows would go after they throwed the Christians to the lions.

And I figured if I went to see the Arab that run it maybe I could start some kind of towel service, the way the fellow at the Moose told me they did in the States, giving people clean towels when they came into the bath, like at a bathing beach. The fellow at the Moose told me that was a big thing in the laundry business.

The women went to the bath before twelve o'clock and the men went after that so when I had some lunch

I went over. It was sure a picture seeing that big room with all the Arab men throwing hot water on themselves under them stone arches three feet thick that looked like they was built before Christ come. With all the steam rising up and the men all naked it looked like a moving picture I seen once where the people were trying to cool themselves in Hell. And I could see they were using plenty of towels.

But the people that come there brought their own, and the Arab wasn't interested.

Louie said I wouldn't get anywhere until I got some of the big Arabs to coming. But how I'd do that I just couldn't figure.

And then I had some luck. There was a big Arab in Bab-El-Kebir they call a caid that I always used to see sitting around the cafés with the police chief or some of the French officers. He was a nice polite fellow and always said "Bon jour"—that's French for hello—whenever I passed him in the street. And one afternoon he came in with his servant that was carrying a couple of bundles and he gave us half a dozen fancy burnooses to be dry-cleaned and a lot of the kind of shirts and things they wear underneath to be washed. Seems like the French governor or somebody was coming to the oasis, and course this big Arab had to meet him, and I guess he wanted to look as nice as he could.

Course this was just what I'd been waiting for, and I dry-cleaned the burnooses myself, and told the Arab women to wash the shirts especially careful, and then the women hung all the clothes on some lines tied to some palm trees along the street back of the laundry. The washing hadn't been there but a few minutes when a man came by driving a bunch of goats, and the goats got scared of a truck and broke away and some of them ran toward the clotheslines and began pulling down the shirts and things every which way.

I pretty near died when I saw the goats doing that to the big Arab's clothes, and I rushed out to make them stop. But the goats were faster than me. I don't know whether they eat clothes like people say, or whether they're just the same as a dog goes after anything that's flapping. Anyway they'd have had those clothes all tramped to pieces if it hadn't been for a young Arab girl that seen the goats charging down and drove them off.

I came up when she was starting to leave. I'd seen her a lot of times in the oasis because she went past the laundry every day, on her way to work for some of the French families cleaning and cooking, and she always reminded me of a bird. It looked like she never walked; she just kind of flew along, she was always so gay and happy.

Course I thanked her plenty for what she'd done.

It was the first time I'd seen her close. She was just a kid, maybe sixteen, but she sure was pretty. She was wearing a blue Arab dress with kind of gold embroidered around the edges, like what I seen on gypsies. She had a blue turban around her brown hair and a wide leather belt around her waist with silver nails and a silver buckle. Her hands and bare feet were awful small and were all painted up with a red stuff they call henna. She had a little nose and mouth, too. But her brown eyes were big and soft as a deer's, with long, dark lashes.

"I would like to work for you," she said in French. "I have done much laundry for the French ladies here. I do not wash with the rocks."

Her voice was nice, too, kind of like a bird singing, and then she started telling me the families she worked for.

"You can ask these French ladies if I do good laundry, *patron*," she said. *Patron* is the French word for boss. "Madame Delacroix, the wife of the Colonel of the Spahis, says when I wash her tablecloths they are white enough to set before the Governor himself."

I was thinking what to do about it, when just then one of the goats come around again, and this Arab girl flew off, chasing it down the street. The big bracelets she had on her arms and around her ankles kept hitting together and playing a kind of tune you could hear till she went around the corner.

She came back in a few minutes, out of breath and all excited. "He is gone now, *patron*," she said. "He will not come back soon. I drove him all the way to the other side of the market."

She looked at the clothes on the lines and saw a big dirty spot from a goat hoof on one of the burnooses.

She turned to me, kind of half worried, half hopeful. "Let me show you how I can wash it, *patron*," she asked me. "The Colonel Delacroix is leaving Bab-El-Kebir, and I do not have a good place to work any longer. If I wash the burnoose well maybe you will let me wash for you."

Well, the old woman that looked like a Chinese was wanting to quit, so I let this girl take the burnoose over to the tub. And she washed it white as snow. And then she stood there, kind of anxious, waiting to find out what I'd say. I guess she needed the work bad.

I couldn't see no reason why not, so I told her I'd give her the job.

And her big brown eyes got little stars in them and

then they went kind of milky. And a awful sweet smile come over her face, like the smile on the statue of the lady I seen on the wall once in a Catholic church when a cowboy buddy of mine that was a Catholic died and I went to the funeral. Her name, she said, was Aziza and I could say that all right.

The fat woman quit right after the old one, and Louie got a pretty Bedouin girl in her place, had earrings big as saucers and heavy brass kind of padlocks around her feet.

Business went a little better after Aziza come. A few other Arabs brought in things to be cleaned, mostly rugs and cushion covers they wanted to sell to the tourists. But it still wasn't nearly enough to keep me going. And things began getting bad again. And then the Arab with the purple turban that'd lent me the money started coming around every day asking me to give it back. And course I couldn't give him a dime.

The Arab said it was twice as much as two hundred dollars now, it was four hundred, and I didn't believe him. Louie had told me not to borrow the money, that he was a terrible crook, and said we'd better go down to the police station and see if Monsieur Dumont could do anything. So we went down and I showed him the copy of the paper I signed. And he twisted his big mustaches and told me, like Louie did, that the Arab was the worst crook in Algeria, and the paper said I've got to pay four hundred dollars what they call on demand.

I went back to the laundry and the fellow with the purple turban was waiting inside with a kind of Arab lawyer. They were looking all around like they already owned the place, and figuring in Arab on a piece of paper.

The moneylender turned to me when I come in and I

noticed something I never had before. His black beard was as sharp and pointed as a knife blade. It looked like it could cut out your heart.

"I do not wish to be unkind, monsieur," he said. "But I need these dollars which you owe me very badly. I will give you until next Friday to pay. If by that time I do not have this money, I will be compelled to take everything in your laundry. And of course your automobile—how do you call it, a jeep?—this I must take also."

After they were gone I counted up my money to see how close I could come maybe to the four hundred. And even when I sold a German pistol I had and a couple of cartons of American cigarettes I sure hated to give up, all I could collect was twenty-six dollars and thirty cents.

I was standing in front of the laundry next day, feeling like the end of the world. I'd got a letter that morning from Ma and she told me she was reading every book and magazine she could get hold of about Algeria so she'd know how to act when she got there. The last time she'd seen the doctor, she said, he told her maybe she ought to go out to Arizona and she said she couldn't, she was going to live with me in North Africa. And the doctor said that was wonderful because Arizona ain't in it with North Africa for the asthma.

She even said she was writing off to a mail-order place in Chicago pricing one of them African helmets. Now I'd have to tell her she couldn't come at all, that it was like the grocery again, and I'd lost everything.

I was thinking how there wasn't anything left now but to close up in a few days and go back to the States, and I was trying to figure whether I'd take up driving a taxi again or go back to the Parts Department, when I see a big crowd gathering in front of a Arab store a little way down the street where they sell jewelry and souvenirs, and pretty soon all of them start hollering and screaming.

And after a while the hollering stops and then I notice a American coming down the road. He's a rich tourist that's been around the oasis a few days sightseeing and spending plenty of money. I'd talked to him a couple of times in the hotel and you could tell right away he was a big fellow, like the man I met at the Moose. Only now he was white as plaster.

He stopped like he recognized me and started shaking so bad I thought he was going to faint.

I held his arm so he wouldn't fall.

"You better come in and sit down a minute," I said. "You're looking bad."

He nodded his head, and I took him back of the store and gave him some brandy. You couldn't get any whisky in the oasis.

He took the drink and started shaking like a leaf again. "I'm in terrible shape," he said.

"What you done?" I asked. "You run over somebody in your auto?" Because I seen him going around in a big, expensive car.

"It's worse than that," he said, wiping his forehead where the sweat's pouring off just like he was taking a bath. "And I didn't mean to do a thing. There was a pretty Arab girl standing in front of that store where they sell jewelry. She can't talk French, but she shows me she'd like one of the bracelets the Arab's got in the window. It didn't cost much, maybe five dollars, and she's a pretty girl, so I gave it to her. And she kisses my hand and starts talking to me in Arab, and then kisses my hand over and

42

hair the way Ma used to do a chicken over the fire before she put it in the oven.

The sandstorms were coming now, besides, and the air'd be so thick it was like yellow smoke blowing everywhere. No matter how tight you shut the doors and windows the sand'd come through and get in your eyes and your coffee and everything till you felt like you were eating sandpaper.

It was hard on the clothes in the laundry, too, getting them all stained and gritty when they were pretty and clean, and soon as the storm stopped they'd have to be washed over. When that happened I was sure glad I'd give the job to Aziza. She'd go flying back and forth, shaking out the sand from the sheets and things, and putting them in the tubs again and running them through the mangle, singing to herself and chattering all the time.

Besides being a fine worker she was sure nice to have around. Sometimes when she came to work she brought a lady's drum, looked like a fancy vase you keep flowers in back home, and when we stopped for lunch she'd play it and sing, and Louie and the Bedouin girl would sing with her.

And then she started bringing a baby goat that she had for a pet the way some of the Arabs did, and she'd carry it under her arm from her house and tie it outside the laundry. And it'd stand there all day maaing.

Aziza was really smart, too. She could what they call parlay French as good as any Frenchman, and she was fine with the customers. She reminded me plenty of times of the girl that worked in the diner where the cabdrivers ate in San Antonio, the one I read the poem to. That girl could cook a plate of ham and eggs for one driver, and make another a steak, and hand out two malted milks, and give four other men cups of coffee all at once. She was on her toes every minute, and Aziza was the same way.

Aziza was a funny girl. Most of the time, like I said, she was happy and smiling. But then all of a sudden she'd get awful serious and seem away off from you, like you wasn't even there. I guess that was the Arab in her.

It was like the Chinese wife of a fellow that made a speech to us one night at the social meeting in the Parts Department who'd been with the Ford Company in Hong Kong and married a Chinese girl. He'd brought her along and I went up and shook hands with her. And she looked straight at you, but it was like she didn't see you or anybody in the room.

Aziza wouldn't stay like the Chinese girl long, though. The next minute she'd be smiling and talking away just like any of the little girls I used to go home from school with in Texas before I quit the fifth grade.

All the Arabs loved flowers and she liked them more than anybody else. Every day she'd come with a almond blossom or a piece of jasmine pinned on her dress. And perfume was the same way. We'd all be going through the market after work and she'd stop in front of the perfume man and smell maybe twenty or thirty bottles before she decided. And then she'd put down a French penny, and get a drop behind each ear, like the kids back home'd buy a cent's worth of gum drops.

She was fine with clothes, too. Course she was awful poor. I paid her as much as I could, five times more than the other people were paying the Arabs. But it still wasn't nothing. And she'd buy a cheap ribbon and a old piece of cloth some merchant was about ready to throw out. And she'd fix it up and wrap it around her, and she'd look wonderful, like them Arab sultan's daughters I seen in the movies.

The coolest place in the oasis was a little park along the river they called the *Pépinière,* had a few kind of stunted trees and bushes, and once after Aziza and the Bedouin girl had been working awful hard, I took them there with Louie on a picnic. The fat woman and the old one that used to be in the laundry came over once in a while to say hello and get a little something to eat, and they said they'd like to go along, so I invited them, too.

I piled everybody and the goat in the jeep about four o'clock when it was cooling off a little, and drove on out. And we sat around under the trees eating hamburgers and hot dogs and potato salad, just like we used to do at Black Spring. And Aziza took her drum and sang. And then I turned on the radio. I got the Army broadcast good. And Louie and me danced with the ladies—I taught them all how to dance American style—and we all had a fine time.

Like I said, it's a funny country. You couldn't turn around that something queer didn't happen you couldn't figure out.

I'd been dancing with Aziza, and we started walking along the river to watch the Arabs carrying water to the gardens.

Aziza turned her big eyes on me. "Can we go to the cemetery, *patron?*" she asked.

I said sure, though it seemed queer to me to want to go to a cemetery when you're on a picnic. She tied up the goat so it wouldn't run off and we went on over.

It was a awful pitiful place with a little slipper laying on a pile of earth showing where some poor Arab's baby

49

was buried or a broken cane where it was a old man. But Aziza just ran around those graves, happy as she could be.

I don't know, seems like the Arabs and all the people over there across the water, French, German, Italian, and everybody just love a cemetery. They have more fun at a cemetery than we do at a ball game.

There was a big yellow mountain right in back of the river so shiny you'd have swore somebody had poured a big kettle of gold over the top and she stood looking at it a minute.

"Can we climb it a little way, *patron?*" she asked, and course I said yes again.

We started along a path that went up one side, just a trail of yellow rocks and sand. All of a sudden a little bird flew up in front of us, all blue except for a bunch of red feathers on its head, and so shiny it looked like one of those birds made of wax that you wind with a key and they sing in their cage till the spring runs down. It was a cute bird, and then I noticed it was acting different than any bird I ever seen. It flew so near us we could have caught it just by putting out our hands.

It'd start chattering and singing a few feet ahead of us, then come back for a minute and fly around our heads, and then go up the path again, chattering and singing louder than ever. It did this every time we stopped for breath.

Aziza's eyes lit up all excited.

"It is a magic bird, *patron,*" she said. "I have heard of these birds when I listened to the storyteller in the market. It wants us to follow."

We went on a little way and stopped again because it was getting late. The sun goes down fast in Africa, and I didn't want to have Aziza caught on that mountain in the dark with so many poison snakes and all the other things around.

The bird flew back and forth, pretty near going crazy.

"Come on, come on," he said, just as plain as if he was talking.

I was getting kind of winded. But Aziza grabbed me by the hand and pulled me up the path.

"Quick, *patron*. We must follow," she said. "It will lead us to great treasure."

I tell you that bird wouldn't let us stop a second. Aziza's dress got caught in thorn bushes half a dozen times, and I got a tear in my shirt, but we had to keep on going. We climbed behind it, all the way to a bunch of prickly-pear cactus growing out of the yellow rocks at the top. And all of a sudden the bird wheeled around and was gone.

Aziza's eyes got like she was way off in the sky. "It was a magic bird," she said. "I do not know what it means."

We went down the mountain slow, even though it was getting dark. After a thing like that you didn't feel like hurrying.

I don't know what the bird wanted. Some science fellows that come through the oasis a while later looking for oil said it might have been what they call a honey bird that leads people to a tree where there's a beehive and then waits for you to give him some of the honey for showing you the place. But I don't know.

You kind of get to believing in magic in a desert where you can see a big lake maybe five miles wide with boats and canoes and pretty houses all along the shore and then when you get up to the water's edge there's nothing but rocks and sand.

We got back to Louie and the others without any trouble, and I gave what was left of the hamburgers and potato salad to the two old women. We had eat up all the frankfurters, six of them apiece, so there weren't any of them left, only the hamburgers. And then we piled all the people and the goat into the jeep again and went home. Everybody said it was a wonderful picnic and hoped I'd have another one soon.

We went out to the *Pépinière* every chance we had after that, the heat was so bad. I wasn't getting much sleep, even staying on the roof all night. And even after I did doze off, I'd generally wake up a couple of hours before daybreak hearing a flock of goats going by on their way to market. And then out in the desert I'd hear a shepherd playing the flute to his sheep, just like David did in the Bible. And then the sun'd come up and the muezzin'd call the first prayer, and right after you'd hear the bugle sounding reveille for the soldiers in the French fort up on the hill.

And sometimes I'd get up and walk along The Street of the Laughing Camel and see the date sellers sweeping in front of their shops, or maybe I'd stop for a minute to watch a Arab making coffee under a big arch in a Arab coffee house. And then I'd come to the market that'd be full of donkeys braying and camels groaning, and Arabs yelling like you thought they were going to kill each other, but they were only passing the time of day. And you sure wouldn't have been surprised to see that Sultan of Baghdad out of *The Arabian Nights* come walking along looking for a pretty girl to take off to his palace. And then I'd go back to the laundry and get ready for work.

When I was in the rest camp I seen a big sultan from

the desert. They had a parade for him and he come and ate with us. A fellow told me them desert sultans don't eat nothing but milk and dates. I guess maybe it's right because I watched him close. He hardly touched the bean soup or the stew, but when the ice cream come around he took seconds.

Things kept going pretty good. And then one time when I was figuring up the accounts, I noticed that some money was missing from the cash box. And then more money's gone and I began to keep watch. And sure enough one afternoon when Louie ain't expecting me, I come in and I see him taking out some bills. Course I got awful mad and I tell him what I think, how we were friends, and I've always tried to be nice to him, and now when my back is turned he does this to me.

I expected him to start crying, like after he told the Arabs about the beans in the jar. But he wasn't sorry at all.

"No, no, Joe," he said. "I don't steal from you this time. This time it is good."

Course that just made me madder. "What you mean you didn't steal?" I said. "I saw you take the money out of the box. I saw it with my own eyes."

His little monkey face got very serious under his red hat. "I tell you this was not stealing, Joe. I stole from you a month ago when we went to the mosque at Sidi-Asa-Din and I told you the price of the fare was four hundred francs, and the fare was really only one hundred. And two weeks before that I stole from you the day when you thought you had lost five hundred francs from a hole in your pocket. It was I who took this money after it fell out of the hole. I made the hole with my knife. But this time it is not stealing. This time it is for Miss Peckham."

He stopped talking a minute to shoo out a camel a Bedouin was driving that started backing through the door. "The people at Fall River in Massachusetts have not sent the little paper this month which she changes for money at the bank. I do not know the reason. Miss Peckham does not tell me. But she has become very unhappy. And this unhappiness makes her also very sick. And she eats nothing. I have taken some of your money from the cashbox to buy her the vegetables of the French which she has liked in the market, the squash and the artichokes, so that maybe she will eat and feel better. So this is not stealing. This is charity. And charity is blessed of Allah."

I hadn't talked to Miss Peckham for almost a month, and I thought she hadn't looked too well last time I saw her. Like I said, I ain't much for going to church, but after all she was the only other American in the oasis, and she sure reminded me of Ma and Black Spring. It made me feel real bad that she was in trouble.

"You ought to have told me," I said.

He kind of shrugged his shoulders. "It was easier to take the money," he answered.

As soon as I could I went over to the Mission.

Louie had gone there ahead of me and opened the door when I knocked. He spoke to me very quiet. "I have not been here since yesterday," he said. "She was very sick in the night. I am afraid maybe she is going to die."

I went inside and after a couple of minutes Miss Peckham came out.

I was shocked when I saw her. Before she'd had little wrinkles in her face kind of like the lines in a leaf after it's been laying on the ground a while. But now they were so deep they looked like they'd been cut with a chisel. And her body was so thin she looked like she wouldn't weigh any more than the ostrich feathers on the wall a missionary had brought her from the desert.

"Sit down and have some tea," she said.

Her smile was nice as ever, but you could see it kind of hurt her to talk. She kept fanning herself with a old black lace fan like the kind I seen in the Spanish bullfight pictures.

She noticed I was worried, I guess.

"The heat is very bad in Bab-El-Kebir this summer," she said. "It is the worst I remember."

She poured me a cup of tea.

"Have you had any word from America on your radio?" she asked. "I have not heard from Fall River for a long time. And I have not received the Fall River paper. I have heard rumors of a hurricane or some other disaster in America. Has there perhaps been an earthquake or a tidal wave in Fall River like that which struck Galveston? I have always worried about a tidal wave at Fall River."

She started to pass me the sugar, and her hand was so shaky the bowl fell to the floor. I scooped up the sugar and put it back on the table.

She looked at me kind of apologetic. Then her eyes filled with tears.

"I am not well," she said. "Last Sunday for the first time since I came to Bab-El-Kebir I did not teach the Sunday School classes or hold Divine Services in the church. I am afraid the Lord does not smile on my work here any longer. I think perhaps the Lord has decided it is time for a useless old woman like me to end her days."

I drank the tea and hurried with Louie over to a Arab house along the river where the French doctor lived that'd come there for his health a long time ago. He was a gray-haired old fellow with a beard and wore big gold glasses tied by a ribbon to his coat.

He took us out to the garden where he had a little stone place with a fountain under the palms, because the office was terrible hot.

"Miss Peckham was in to see me this morning," he said. "I have known Miss Peckham since she first came to the oasis. She is not physically sick. Miss Peckham's sickness is mental."

It was hot even in the garden and he kept wiping his beard and hair all the time with a handkerchief. "Miss Peckham is worried about the money that has not come from the church. But that is not her real concern. That worry will pass when the check arrives. It has probably been delayed in the mail. The trouble is that it has set her to thinking and now she sees all her life as a failure. She has lost her motive for living. The cure Miss Peckham needs is some converts to her faith. She is a very frail old woman. Unless she gets some convert other than your worthless Mohammed here, I am afraid her hours are numbered."

We went out of the house. I could see Louie's face was drawn all tight the way it always looked when he was thinking hard.

I got back to the laundry just as the muezzin was calling the prayer for sunset and started to cook myself some eggs for supper. It was too hot to eat anything heavy.

And there was a knock at the door and I see Louie with two Arab men, terrible bums with beards and ragged burnooses that hung around the oasis and were drunk most of the time. The Arabs ain't allowed to drink according to

56

the Arab Bible they call the Koran, so when they start taking liquor it's bad. And there was a kind of skinny Arab girl in a green dress with them that was one of the worst tramps in town.

Louie motions them inside.

"What's the idea?" I said to him quiet so they can't hear. "Why you bringing those bums and that tramp here?"

"They're Miss Peckham's new converts," he answered. "I told them you'd pay them each twenty-five francs, ten cents a day anyway, till her next check comes. And they said all right. If you want to, we can take them over to her right away."

I was worried she wouldn't believe them for a minute. But Louie said he was the only one she had to depend on. She always believed anything he said. I guess you can tell anything to a old lady seventy-six living by herself in a oasis in Africa. But just so there wouldn't be too many of them and get her suspicious I made him send the skinny girl home.

"Maybe before we go, you could teach them some of the Lord's Prayer, Joe," Louie tells me. "If they could say a few words of the Lord's Prayer with her it would make Miss Peckham very happy."

I worked with them for a hour the way he wanted but they weren't very smart. All I could get them to do was to kind of mumble "Father in Heaven."

We started out for the Mission. Louie stopped in the road just before we went inside and turned to the two Arabs. His face was all tight again.

"You remember you are going to be good Christians," he said. "If you do not, I will not give you a sou. And I will

57

also tell Monsieur Dumont how you get the money for the wine you drink by selling hashish for the Arab that comes here from Tangiers."

They nodded, and Louie went up and knocked.

Miss Peckham looked puzzled when she came to the door and saw the two Arabs with us.

"These have been evil men," Louie said. "They wish to come to the Lord, like me."

Miss Peckham kind of quivered for a minute. Then her face got like the time I was driving a cab and I took a old foreign lady out to the airport and she seen her daughter coming who'd been in one of them awful German camps and everybody thought she was dead. She began to pray.

A minute later she took us into the kitchen. She spread a cloth on the table and began putting out all kinds of things she took from a cupboard.

Louie moved up some chairs. The two Arabs sat down kind of uneasy.

Miss Peckham bowed her head.

"Before we eat let us recite the Lord's Prayer," she said.

Louie began to repeat the words after her and kicked the Arabs under the table. They kind of mumbled "Father in Heaven," over and over.

Miss Peckham looked up at the stars showing through the trap door in the roof.

"Thank you, Lord, for this miracle," she said.

CHAPTER SEVEN

IT WAS LIKE the French doctor told us, the money from
Fall River came along in a week or so, three checks together.

Miss Peckham was feeling a lot better now. But the two
Arabs were kind of slowing up, and we didn't want her to
go back the way she was before.

The doctor had told me she ought to get out where she
could see and talk to people, that it was being by herself
so much that was so hard on her. But where you were
going to take Miss Peckham in Bab-El-Kebir sure wasn't
easy.

Lots of people went to the cafés, but they were all soldiers, pretty near, and there weren't no ladies at all. Anyway you couldn't take her there because she thought liquor come straight from the devil.

There was one place where ladies did go and that was down to the Ouleds in the afternoon to have tea. Course I told you about the Ouleds. But there wasn't anywhere else.

I mentioned the Ouleds to her one day and said I'd take her if she'd like to go.

She turned pale.

"I have read of the sinful ways of the Ouleds even before I left Fall River," she said. "They are the daughters of Jezebel. I could not enter the dwelling of these women and ever face my Lord again."

I kept talking to her, though, and so did Louie. We told her how everybody that came to the oasis went there, the Governor and his wife and all the big people. And then Louie told her that it looked to him it was her duty to go, that maybe if she went she could get them to live different, and maybe get them to come to the Mission.

I could see she was getting interested, and one day when I came with Louie she was all dressed up in her best black dress and her little black hat.

Her eyes looked like she hadn't done any sleeping, and her lips were kind of stiff and white, like when you've decided something hard.

"I talked with the Lord last night," she said. "He wishes me to go to the house of the Ouleds. I am ready now."

We walked to the middle of the town and then turned down a narrow street that led off to the square where the Ouleds lived. Lemonade sellers were walking up and down, making funny cries, and beggars were holding out their bowls, and a man was sitting in a doorway playing a bagpipe. The houses were so close together they almost touched over your head. You had to stand sideways pretty near to let the other people pass.

We'd gone a little way when who do I see coming along toward us but Monsieur Dumont, the chief of police, smoking like a stove you've put too much polish on. He stopped and looked shocked when he sees us, and asked me where we were going.

I told him we were taking Miss Peckham to the Ouleds, and he almost bit through one of his mustaches.

"You will get me into terrible trouble, my friend," he said.

We squeezed on past him and a minute later I looked back and he was still standing there, looking after Miss Peckham and shaking his head.

We got to the square with the Ouled houses around, all adobe, with iron balconies on the second story. It looked kind of like Mexico. Some of the girls were out in front, all covered with their jewels, and there were a lot of Arab soldiers and some old Arab women wearing veils.

We stopped in front of the biggest house that was the place where the guides always took the tourists and their wives. Miss Peckham stood looking around a minute, kind of shivering. Her lips were moving a little and I figured she was praying. Then she walked toward the door.

"I will go in the house now," she said.

We went inside and a big stout Ouled with red hair, maybe about fifty, that was a friend of Louie's came to meet us. I could tell she was kind of surprised to see Miss

Peckham, because she knew who Miss Peckham was, but she was awful nice to her, and showed us into a big room with fancy Arab rugs on the floor and the walls.

It was like some of the places I seen once in Dallas when the Shriners gave a circus. There were maybe half a dozen young Ouleds sitting around on big Arab cushions, laughing and chattering. They were all as surprised as the red-headed woman to see Miss Peckham, but they did everything to be nice, too. One of them brought her a cushion, and then they hurried around bringing her tea, and one of them brought her a plate of honey cakes, and another brought a dish of candied fruit.

They were pretty little things, like I said. Whenever they sat still they looked just like idols.

Miss Peckham was awful stiff at first, and stayed on her cushion like she was made of iron. But the girls kept running around, cute as puppies, smiling and touching her with their little hands when they passed her more tea or brought some Arab candy, and pretty soon she began talking to them, and it wasn't long before she was smiling, too.

And then Louie asked them to dance and the redheaded woman went into a back room, and a minute later a old fellow come in with a flute and another with a drum, and they sat down and began to play. And the girls did a dance like you see in some of them Hindu travel pictures—making all kinds of angles with their hands and jerking their necks till you'd think their heads'd snap off. People told me they were religious dances.

Miss Peckham got like iron again when they started the dancing, but when she saw the kind of dance it was she sat back with her hands in her lap, looking very happy.

"It's beautiful," she said when they finished. "It's like a lovely painting."

I had worried how to get her down to the Ouleds in the first place, but now I was worried how to get her out. She liked it so well she didn't want to leave. Some tourists came in from the hotel and the girls did the dance again, and then I saw the guide talking to the fat woman, and I knew he was saying the tourists wanted to see them dance naked, the way they always did when you paid them extra. And that dance wasn't what you call religious.

The old fellows that played the drum and the flute got all ready, and the naked dance was going to begin. And Louie and me knew we had to get her out of there in a hurry.

So I said I had some rush work over at the laundry that couldn't wait. And she told the girls and the fat woman good-by, and gave each of them a little Bible and some Sunday School cards, and we went outside.

"They are sweet girls," she said, when we were crossing the square in front. "I wish the Lord would help me make them part of my flock at the Mission. I must write to my friends in Fall River and tell them the stories I read in the books there are not true."

We took her down to see the Ouleds three or four times a week after that. And she began looking better than we'd ever seen her, with the wrinkles in her face all smoothed out. Every time she came she brought the girls little presents, crocheted things the church people had sent her from New England, little tablecloths and what they call doilies and aprons and dishcloths and frying-pan holders and toast racks and things like that. Course, she'd always give them Bibles and Sunday School cards, too.

And the girls took them all and next time they'd have presents for her, a beautiful pair of slippers maybe, or a embroidered scarf, or maybe a fancy cushion. And then they'd sing Arab songs and I'd start up my radio I'd brought over from the laundry, and play some hillbilly music or swing that we'd get on the Army broadcast.

But we always hurried her out of there before seven o'clock because that was when the tourists generally started coming and the naked dancing could begin any time.

We had a few kind of close shaves in the Ouled house. Once when we were there a Arab tried to rob a Ouled of all the jewelry she was wearing, and she ran out in the square and the fat woman ran out to help her and there was a terrible fight with a lot of yelling and screaming, and we had to tell Miss Peckham there was a bad automobile accident.

We were walking back from the Ouled house one day, when Miss Peckham turned to me. "I have had tea with the Ouleds here so many times it would make me very happy to have them for tea at the Mission," she said. "I know they are Mohammedans and will not attend the church. But perhaps if I tell them this is merely a social visit to show my appreciation of their kindnesses they would be willing to come."

I wasn't sure she could do it, because I didn't know if the police chief would give the Ouleds a permit to leave the Ouled square. Whenever they went away from there the chief had to give them a paper. But Miss Peckham asked the girls and they said they'd go, so I went to see Mr. Dumont at the police station. He looked awful worried again but he gave me the paper all right, and Miss

Peckham fixed up the time for the afternoon two days later.

Well, it was sure something seeing me and Louie going down to the house of the Ouleds and coming out with those girls. It was like a parade in the Army. Louie and me were in front, and then came the fat woman dressed up all in red like her hair so she looked like a fire wagon, and then behind her came eleven of the Ouleds, all shining with their gold necklaces and bracelets so they looked like a jewelry store window. Some of the girls were giggling, and some of them were awful solemn, like they were going to a funeral. Course, we had to walk all the way across town, and with the Arabs and the French people all standing and staring, wondering what was going on, I sure felt awful foolish.

We got them to the Mission all right. Miss Peckham gave them tea and cakes and strawberry preserves and candy and things like that. She always gave you plenty to eat. And they sat around and talked, and she showed them a photograph album of her family, and books with pictures of things back in the States.

She looked at the girls kind of doubtful. "Would you care to see some stereoptican slides?" she asked. "I have some beautiful slides of Yellowstone Park sent me by my friends in Fall River."

Course they said yes. And she took out a kind of magic lantern looked like she'd got it when she first started the Mission.

Louie put in a slide for her and clicked out the lights.

"This picture is what we call Old Faithful Geyser," she said, reading with a flashlight from a card she was holding. "It is one of God's most glorious works of Nature that hurls itself high into the air every sixty-five minutes. It never fails us. It is God's lesson to us that we must be dependable."

She showed a lot more slides and after that the girls got ready to go home. Miss Peckham gave them each some cakes and candy to take along and a beautiful silk handkerchief. She started to give them Sunday School cards but then she remembered she'd given her word she wouldn't, and she put them away again, though I could see it was hard for her to do it. And then Louie and me lined up the parade again, and took them back to the house of the Ouleds.

Miss Peckham was getting along fine, and then one day she got word from the States that a man named Liggett, one of the big missionary fellows of her church in the States, was coming over to look at the missions in Africa, and was going to stop and see her in Bab-El-Kebir.

I was kind of worried because I knew my uncle that was the Holiness preacher wouldn't have liked the Ouleds and maybe this fellow'd be the same kind. But then she said he wasn't coming until a couple of months when he'd be on his way back from the Congo, so I didn't think about it too much.

Well, it wasn't long after Miss Peckham had the Ouleds up to the Mission the girls decided they ought to give her a little party the same way. So we took her down to the house, and the girls sang and danced, and the redheaded woman told Miss Peckham how much they all loved her, and gave her a beautiful rug the girls had wove on a loom with their own hands. And she was so happy she could hardly thank them she was so near crying. And they were all crowded around her, talking away, when all of a sudden there's a terrible racket outside and a giant of a fellow dressed all in black like a undertaker comes rushing in, and his eyes are blazing red like a bull. If it'd been dark, I'll bet they'd have showed like balls of fire, the way a alligator's eyes do when you shine them with a flashlight in a swamp.

I didn't need more than one look to know it's Mr. Liggett, the big missionary from America.

He sees Miss Peckham, and goes past Louie and me and the Ouleds like we wasn't there, and he grabs Miss Peckham by the arm.

"Out of this house of abomination!" he roars. And he jerks her out of the room like she was a bomb somebody throwed that was going to blow everything up. And just by bad luck, some tourists had come down early from the hotel and some of the girls were in the other room dancing for them without any clothes on, and Mr. Liggett and Miss Peckham couldn't help going right past.

I ran to the door of the house and looked out and I could see he still had her by the arm and was rushing her across the square like he was crazy.

Well, it was awful. I found out later what'd happened. Mr. Liggett had stopped on his way going down to the Congo, instead of on his way back, and the Arab girl that worked over at the Mission sometimes told him where Miss Peckham was visiting. Mr. Liggett was so wild he left on the first plane out in the morning.

Miss Peckham took it better than I thought. I saw her next day, and she was holding herself as stiff as them rich ladies I used to drive when I was cabbing in San Antonio and they seen their husbands making a fuss over another woman.

"Whatever anyone tells me, they are fine girls," she said. "This Mr. Liggett may be a man of the cloth. But the cloth has not taught him humility. I do not think my church in Fall River would care to deprive these poor children of the services of a woman of God."

She fixed up a big bundle of Bibles and Sunday School cards, and asked us to take her to the house of the Ouleds again. Course we did what she wanted, but it wasn't the same any more, and after a few times she stopped going altogether.

I guess it was maybe a month or so later I was working in the laundry when Monsieur Dumont come hurrying in to talk to me. I could see he was so worried he wasn't even smoking.

"I said you would get me into terrible trouble, my friend," he tells me. "Look at this. It is the Algiers paper of this morning."

He put the paper down in front of me and all I can see is a headline running across the front page about a big scandal among the Ouleds in Bab-El-Kebir. He looks at me like a prairie dog one time I was cowboying and I pulled up a fence post that was the back of her hole where she was all comfortable with a litter of pups and now she'd have to dig her hole all over.

"Why have you done this to me, my friend?" he said. "Do I not have enough trouble with hashish smugglers and black markets and counterfeit money? This mad missionary Liggett has arrived in London and he has given an interview to the English newspapers about the dreadful moral conditions here in Bab-El-Kebir. You know the English, they never miss a chance to talk about our morals. Just as if the Ouleds were French, not Arabs. The

Minister of Security in Paris has called the head of the Police Administration, and the head of the Police Administration has called the head of the police in Algeria, and the head of the police in Algeria has just telephoned me. This is likely to cost me my job."

Course they all forgot about it in a little while, everybody except Miss Peckham. A couple of times when she'd get a box from the States she'd send the Ouleds little presents. And she'd ask me about the redheaded woman and the other girls. And she could hardly say the words, her voice'd get so choky.

CHAPTER EIGHT

IT STARTED COOLING OFF NOW, and pretty soon it got so you could sleep inside again. But it seemed like hot or cool the laundry business didn't get any better.

There were a lot of people in the big hotel, though, and plenty of Americans, and like before some of them saw the *New York Laundry* sign outside and came over. A couple of times there were people from Texas, and once there was even a fellow from San Antonio. And we sat around and talked and I asked him how things were on Commerce Street and he said they were fine.

It turned out he rode a cab a couple of times a week with a driver that was a friend of mine, had a big scar on his left cheek he got in a fight with a Mexican. We called the driver Scarface, for the scar. The fellow's name from San Antonio was Cox. But I never met anybody from Black Spring.

I was behind the counter one day not long after meeting the San Antonio man when a big dark fellow looks like a Spaniard comes in wearing a expensive suit and a big diamond ring on his finger and smoking a fancy cigarette. He looks around kind of smart aleck.

"How's tricks, New York?" he asks.

"Okay," I answered. "You from the States?"

Even though he looks like a Spaniard he talked like one of them fellows from New York I met while we were in camp in New Jersey.

He took a puff of the cigarette. "I'm from Cairo, Egypt," he said. "But I've been in New York plenty. I had a restaurant there for ten years in Prohibition, but I was really bootlegging. What you doing here? Selling dope?"

"I'm running a laundry," I said. "If you can read the 'New York,' I guess you can read the 'Laundry.'"

I was kind of sarcastic, because I didn't like his looks.

He shrugged his shoulders. "I thought it was a racket," he said. "Everybody in North Africa's got a racket."

I saw he was after something.

"What's on your mind?" I said, kind of sharp again.

I can be kind of nasty when I want to, like a couple of times when I was a cowboy and I had to quiet down a mean drunk in a saloon.

His eyes got kind of slippery.

"There's big money in it for you," he said. "Me and my partners in Cairo got plenty. It's black market. Running penicillin and diamonds and a few guns maybe. The French police watch us pretty close, but they wouldn't follow an American so quick. . . . How about us cutting you in?"

"Don't slam the door when you go out," I told him.

71

He grins at me. "No hard feelings," he said. "Everybody in North Africa's got a racket."

He started toward the door.

"I'll be seeing you," he said, and flashed the big diamond on his finger and went up the street.

He got me mad, especially because things now wasn't going so good. But I guess you can't figure what them Egyptians 'll do. I saw a movie about Cleopatra and the Egyptians once. She was giving a big banquet and right in the middle she stung herself with a snake.

Well, business kept on going down. The Bedouin girl quit to go off with her family in the desert and I was glad to see her leave because there hadn't been enough laundry for two girls and I'm the kind that hates to fire anybody.

Course I still had Aziza, and even if there had been a lot of business, she could have handled it all right, she was so smart. And she was sure good company. Sometimes after we got through work, Aziza and me and Louie'd walk out to the French fort on the hill. And she'd hop up the path going to the top, and the goat would hop after her, and you could hardly tell which jumped better, the goat or Aziza. Or we'd go up the winding stairs to the mosque tower and sit and talk with the muezzin that was one of Louie's friends. Funny, Aziza being a girl, she couldn't go inside the mosque, but they let her come up on the roof that way all right.

And we'd look out over the oasis, and then the muezzin started calling out to Allah and we could see the caravans and everybody stop wherever they were and get down on their knees and start praying. And then in a few minutes we'd see the caravans moving on again, maybe to Timbuktu.

And sometimes we'd all take a walk in the desert at night with the moon shining, and all of a sudden I'd see a shadow moving over the sand, and it'd be a hyena slipping past on his way to dig up a grave. Or we'd come on the skeleton of a camel so white it looked like it was made out of plaster, and then you'd see a long snake wriggling off, the same kind of snake they had in the movie that killed Cleopatra. And you'd think about her and the Queen of Sheba and the Arabs and all those people and how they'd been living out here in this sand for thousands of years, long before anybody ever heard of America or Black Spring. And it made you feel all funny inside.

Wherever we went Aziza'd always be seeing some kind of sign that meant good luck or bad luck, like a big lizard coming in the house meant you were going to get a lot of money or seeing a scorpion on its back meant you were going to die. She was awful superstitious, like all the other Arabs.

One day I was coming down the street toward the laundry, and I saw smoke rolling out the window. I thought the place was on fire and I ran inside to put it out. But instead of a fire I saw Aziza and a girl that lived next door each standing over one of the little clay pots of charcoal I had on the stove for my cooking, watching the smoke roll up and laughing and giggling. Sparks were flying everywhere and there was a smell like when you light Chinese punk on the Fourth of July.

I asked them what they were doing.

"We are burning incense, *patron*," Aziza told me, giggling again. "We did not think you would be back to see. It is to bring us a good husband."

Course I laughed, too, and went off to fix something.

73

And then all of a sudden I heard a crash and Aziza gave a little cry. And I turned around and I saw the pot in front of her had broke in two, with the heat, I guess, and the red coals were spilling all over the stove.

Aziza turned pale.

I started scooping up the charcoal so it wouldn't fall on some of the clothes maybe and start a fire sure enough.

"What's the matter?" I asked. "You didn't hurt anything."

She stood there looking miserable. "The pot has broken," she said. "It is a terrible sign. I will have an unhappy marriage."

I told her it didn't mean a thing, that when people said things like that they were just doing it for foolishness. And I got her cheered up fast. And pretty soon she forgot all about it and she was running around the laundry as gay as ever.

Miss Peckham liked Aziza a lot, too, and pretty often me and Aziza and Louie would go over to see her. And Aziza would play a kind of Arab mandolin they call a lute and sing a Arab song and Louie would play the flute. And then Aziza would dance, not like the Ouleds, but just swaying soft and slow, like a palm tree bending in the breeze. And then maybe she'd tell one of them *Arabian Nights* stories about a giant coming out of a bottle or a prince being turned into a butterfly or a lizard. I tell you when you had that Aziza around you didn't need to go to a show.

A couple of times Louie and me went over to Aziza's house. It was a poor little place, kind of like the adobe houses the Mexicans have in Texas, and was 'way out at the edge of town. In front there was a skinny camel and a donkey tied up that her father rented for carrying wood and things.

The father was a ugly little Arab, had a big wart under one eye, and was grinning all the time; her mother was a little wrinkled woman with a sour face, kind of dried up like the inside of a walnut when the meat ain't good.

You wouldn't have thought those two'd ever have a beautiful girl like Aziza. People sure ain't like horses.

They had a tent a little way off, and they lived there part of the time when it was hot. They had a dog, too, big as a wolf. And he acted like a wolf, the same as the other Arab dogs. They ain't like our dogs. The Arabs have to keep them chained all the time. When you came close to the house or the tent, this dog ran up and down barking like he was crazy, and tearing at his chain to get loose. I guess if he ever did you'd have been done for.

Well, about this time I got another letter from Ma asking when she could come over. And I didn't pay any attention when I wrote her, because it looked like it was going to be never. Fact is, things were getting so bad I began thinking about borrowing from one of the money lenders again.

And then something good happened for a change. A Arab came in that had bought up a lot of surplus Army blankets in Algiers, and was going to sell them down in Ghardaia and other places in the Sahara. He wanted them dry-cleaned before he sold them because he'd get more for them that way, and he said if I gave him a good price he'd give me the job.

I figured things pretty close and I got the work all right. There were blankets coming through every week, and it kept us busier than we'd been any time since I came

75

to the oasis. And I wrote Ma it looked like she'd be coming over pretty soon.

I guess if I hadn't been so busy I'd have found out about the way things was with Aziza sooner. Having just the one girl now I'd got to appreciating her more than ever. The more I seen her the better I liked her.

She was fine handling the laundry money, too, though she sure wasn't good at keeping the little bit of pay I gave her. There wasn't a Armenian peddler come around the store that she didn't buy something, a cheap ring maybe, or a pair of beaded slippers.

And it wasn't only for herself she got things. Plenty of times if I hadn't stopped her she'd have bought me a pair of cuff buttons or a fancy cigarette holder, and once when I wasn't around she bought me a Arab shirt and a red hat must have cost her a whole week's wages. I put on the hat and shirt every once in a while just to please her, and they sure looked funny. If one of the horses I used to ride around Black Spring would have seen me he'd have run all the way to California.

And then all of a sudden she changed. I'd kind of noticed she hadn't been dancing around the way she always did before and didn't wear the flowers or buy perfume or slippers any more. And then one day a Arab stopped by the window and looked at her a long time, a fat oily fellow had a face on him like a pig. He reminded me of a big party they had once out in Texas when they served a whole pig on a tray with two little apples in his eyes.

I'd been seeing him around the oasis a couple of weeks. He was a rich trader that come from Bab-El-Kebir, had a store in what they call Rio de Oro down below Morocco and come back every once in a while to visit his people.

He saw me looking at him when he was watching Aziza, and his pig eyes got kind of embarrassed and he walked away.

A couple of days later Aziza was putting tags on the clean blankets so they wouldn't get mixed up, when I saw her wiping her eyes. And I looked close and saw they were all red and swollen from crying.

I got awful worried. "What's the matter?" I said. "Has Louie or me done something to hurt you?"

She shook her head. "I am going to be married."

Her face got like the time I went to a museum and I seen some statues there they dug up out of the ground thousands of years ago, just kind of cold and dead.

"It is Mama and Papa," she said. "I knew that day when the pot broke with the incense it would happen. They are going to marry me to a merchant who will take me off to the Rio de Oro. He has three wives and he is old and fat. But he is rich and we are very poor."

You could have knocked me over with a feather, the way they say. I'd heard plenty about the Arabs marrying off their daughters without asking whether they liked the fellow or not. People did it all over Africa and lots of places in Europe, too.

But it was different when it happened to somebody you knew and that worked for you, especially a young girl like Aziza who was just sixteen. And the pig-eyed fellow, when I saw him looking through the window, wasn't a day less than fifty.

She didn't say any more, just sat there kind of quiet, with every once in a while a tear trickling down her cheek.

I talked it over with Louie, and we went out to Aziza's house to find the old people. They weren't there, but we saw them in the tent and walked on over. The wild dog was rushing up and down, tearing at his chain, and the old man came out and held him so we could go inside. It was a big tent, kind of smelled of leather the old man was cutting, and the little woman that looked like a bad walnut started fixing tea.

Louie talked to them a long time and I could see his monkey face turning darker and darker. He got up from his cushion at last and we walked toward the door.

"It's finished, Joe," he said. "The old man just told me the merchant has paid the dowry. He will marry her now. This is the Mohammedan law."

I went over to Miss Peckham's and she felt as bad as me.

Things went on like this for a few days. Aziza came to the laundry just the same and did her work as good as ever, but I could see she was crying all the time. One day I heard her singing a song that was so kind of mournful it made you think of all the sad sounds you had ever heard in your life, things like a train whistle blowing on the prairie at night, and the wind moaning before a storm, and a lost calf bleating for its mother, and people singing hymns around your father's grave.

I asked her what the song was about.

She dried her eyes and put some sheets through the mangle. "It is an old song that my mother's mother taught me. She said it is the song of all Arab women. It is about a young girl who must marry an old man because he has bought her for a wife like he would buy a camel or an ox. After she is married, all day she sits by her balcony window and watches the young men passing in the street below. And then one night she lets down her long black hair, hoping one of them will climb up it to her balcony. She does this night after night. And one night she feels someone climbing up and when he reaches her window, she holds out her arms in an embrace. It is not one of the young men, it is her husband with a knife, to kill her for her unfaithfulness. But he does not strike the blow. She is already dead of sorrow. This was the story my mother's mother told. It will be my story, too."

I kept thinking and thinking. And then one afternoon all of a sudden she stopped the work she's doing and sat down on a chair and buried her head in her hands and sobbed till you'd think her little body was going to break. I stood there a minute and I decided.

"I've got a Army buddy over in Tunis," I said to her. "He's married to a Italian girl, and they run a restaurant. I'll drive you there in the jeep and you can stay with her till this blows over."

The sobbing stopped and her head come up. And she gave me a look I'd only seen once before in my life, one time when a mother cat lost some kittens down a broken sewer pipe back of a ranch house and they'd been there three days before I found them and brought them out. It was so kind of happy and pitiful all together it made you shiver.

CHAPTER NINE

I<small>T WAS THE SANDSTORM SEASON AGAIN</small>, and I could tell
from the sky one was coming next day.

I knew this would be a good time to leave, because the
storm would keep the old man busy with the donkey and
the camel.

I went over to Miss Peckham's and told her, and she
gave me some dresses and things she said Aziza'd need
when she was away. I decided I'd leave Louie in Bab-El-
Kebir to keep the laundry running so people wouldn't get
suspicious. I'd been away a couple of times going to
Algiers.

It was a easy trip to Tunis, with good roads all through,

and we could make it by noon easy the next day if we kept traveling all night.

About sunset, just before it was time for Aziza to go home, Louie helped me load up the jeep with some blankets and things so it'd look like we were delivering laundry. And Aziza fed the goat that was tied outside and made Louie promise to look after it while she was gone. And then she climbed in the back seat behind the curtain where nobody'd see her and we started off.

We got out of Bab-El-Kebir all right and soon as it was dark Aziza came up in the front seat and sat by me. She was terrible excited and kept talking every minute, like a bird I seen once in the zoo in San Antonio, chattering its head off because it'd just flew out of its cage.

We went through a little town where a truck was standing at the curb under an electric light. It was full of pigs being taken to the French somewhere, because the Arabs don't eat pork. There was one pig at the end had popeyes and a kind of silly grin, the way some hogs do.

Aziza grabbed my hand and gave one of her little laughs that sounded like those Japanese glass things you hang over a door and the wind makes them ring like bells.

"That was my husband, *patron*," she said.

We left the town and began twisting through some big mountains, with queer-shaped rocks all around us, looked like the Arab castles I seen blown to pieces by air raids in the war. The wind was coming up now, and sand began hitting the car and stinging our eyes. Once in a while some kind of animal crossed the road, and a couple of times back in the shadows of a cave I saw what might be men.

I could hear the bracelets on Aziza's arms start tinkling loud, like she was shivering. I put on the flashlight and she

81

was all drawn up in her gold-embroidered dress, looking awful scared.

"There are terrible bandits in these mountains, *patron*," she said. "They rob the travelers who pass and then cut off their heads."

I patted her hand and told her she'd be all right.

We came near a funny-shaped rock and the headlights showed a big hole in the shape of a man's foot.

Aziza said some words to herself sounded like when the Arabs are praying in a mosque.

"The great prophet, Sidi Abd-El-Kadir, passed here once," she told me. "And he met a bandit who would not bow to Allah when Sidi Abd-El-Kadir told him it was time to say his prayers. Sidi Abd-El-Kadir became angry and stamped his foot against the stone. That was many years ago, but the mark of his foot is still there."

The road kept getting twistier and twistier, and then before I knew it we were out of the mountains, down in the flatland, and I thought the driving would be better. But the wind was blowing harder now and the sand was coming around us till it looked like smoke. I had to stop all the time to clean the windshield so I could see.

It had got terribly hot, too, but I had to keep the jeep curtains shut tight on account of the sand, and you could hardly breathe. It got worse and worse, and pretty soon the sand was so thick the headlights were just kind of red glows. It was like you were trying to drive by a couple of lighted cigar stubs.

All of a sudden I saw something ahead like a ghost, and I slammed on the brakes and we gave a big skid and went rocking off the road. We stopped and I seen that what looked like the ghost was just a camel with half a dozen other camels behind him. They went on up the highway.

I jumped down from the jeep and looked around and saw that all four wheels were deep in the sand. I could have dug out all right, but the storm was so bad I knew if we tried to go on we'd get stuck again every few minutes, so I thought it'd be better to just sit there in the car and wait till daylight.

I could see Aziza was shivering again and I asked her what was the matter.

"It is the bandits, *patron*," she told me. "They are worse here than in the mountains. Before I was born my mother's mother was traveling here with her husband and many others and the bandits came down like the wolves and killed all the caravan. Only my mother's mother and her husband and one other escaped."

I told her not to worry, that I had a pistol.

"A pistol can not harm these bandits, *patron*," she answered. "They are Ifrits, the ghosts of robbers who were killed in the old days by the soldiers of the Sultan. My mother's mother said these Ifrits have a perfume like jasmine to deceive those whom they are going to murder. I smell jasmine strongly. I think there must be an Ifrit near us now."

The sand stopped blowing for a while and the air got clearer. And then I noticed Aziza staring out of the jeep awful hard like she saw something. Her eyes and ears were wonderful sharp, because she'd been living out in the desert most of her life.

She turned to me and her face was all happy.

"It is a cemetery, *patron*," she said. "If we go there we

will be safe. The ghosts of the bandits will not come to a cemetery. For there are holy men in the graves and their ghosts will drive the ghosts of the bandits away."

It sure sounded awful foolish to me. But to make her less scared I went over.

It was a open place with a few graves and a little white stone house where a holy man was buried. The sand began to blow again, but we sat just inside the door of the holy man's house and it didn't touch us. I took out some lunch I'd brought in the car and we ate and talked.

Aziza was all gay again. It was like the day we were out on the picnic in the *Pépinière*.

We sat there till daylight come. The storm ended just about then and we walked over to the jeep. It was all filled up with sand, and the wheels were so deep now you could hardly see the tires. But I got dug out fast, and pretty soon we were rolling across the desert.

I kept watching behind to see if we were being followed, but the road was empty.

Aziza kept looking back all the time like me.

"Do you think my father can come now?" she asked.

"We had a good start," I answered. "And I been driving a long time. If I couldn't get through last night I don't think your father could neither."

She got happier and happier the nearer we got to the border.

"Will you come and visit me sometime in Tunis, *patron?*" she asked all of a sudden.

"Sure, sure," I said, not paying too much attention because now I was trying to make time.

"Will you let me work in the laundry again when I come back?"

"Ain't any doubt about that," I answered.

She looked worried. "Last week I tore a sheet in the mangle belonging to Miss Peckham. I did not tell you because I was afraid you would not let me work in the laundry any more."

Toward noon we began to pass little farms and olive groves, and Arab and French houses. And pretty soon we went through a little town and I saw the customs shed where Algeria ends and you come to the Tunis frontier.

"That's good-by to the pig-eyed man," I said and drove up to the gate.

Just then I noticed a couple of men in shiny uniforms and caps, what they call gendarmes, looking awful hard at Aziza and me, and one of them walked up to the car.

"You must come with me to the police station, monsieur," he said.

We go down the road to a adobe building with a French flag flying over it, and there's another gendarme with a lot of stripes on his sleeve sitting at a desk, studying a telegram.

"Your name is Cullum, monsieur?" he asked me.

I told him that's right.

"I must inform you that you are under arrest, monsieur," he said. "There is an alarm out for you and this girl."

It seems like Aziza's father had told the police in Bab-El-Kebir, and they telegraphed the other police to be looking out for the jeep, the way they do in the States when a robber's escaping, so we didn't have a chance to get away.

Well, the police didn't exactly put me or Aziza in jail. I guess they didn't want to lock up a American. They just made us stay there in the station, sitting in a couple of chairs, not talking or anything, just staring at the wall. I guess we looked as miserable as the poor Mexicans I used to see in the station in San Antonio when I was cabbing, little old men and women all folded up in their shawls and blankets, arrested for stealing a couple of cans of beans maybe, and with faces like they didn't have a friend in the world.

Pretty soon a old Arab man that looked more like the inside of a bad walnut than Aziza's mother come in with a couple of Arab women all covered with veils, and they took Aziza away from me, and hurried her off into a room at the back and I could hear them talking to her awful mad. The gendarme with the stripes told me he was her uncle or something, though she hadn't seen him since she was a little girl. He said her father had got the police there to tell the old man to come over.

The Arabs in the other room kept on scolding Aziza, and the women began kind of crying, and they come out, with Aziza in the middle, all huddled up around her like hens trying to keep rain off a young chicken, and they hurried out the door and down the street. And then a policeman took me off to a run-down little hotel a few doors away, and told me I'd have to stay there until the U.S. Consul come, and not to go out of the hotel till they sent for me.

The gendarme had been gone a hour or so when a bunch of Arabs, men and women both, began collecting outside and shook their fists at me where they could see me sitting by the window, and began hollering, and I guess they were saying what they'd do to me as soon as they got the chance. Some of them were carrying knives and daggers in their belts. And every once in a while they'd pull the knives out and go like they were cutting my throat.

It was just like the time Louie got the money out of the rich fellow from Michigan, only this time it was real. I don't know what the Arabs figured I'd done. They kept it up until they got too bad and a policeman come over from the station and made them go away.

I stayed in the hotel till next afternoon, and then the gendarme came and took me over to the police station again. The place was full of people now, Aziza, and her mother and father that had come in from Bab-El-Kebir, and the old uncle with the two women, and a couple of Arab lawyers and a fellow they said was a cadi, that's a kind of Arab judge, and I don't know what all.

The French chief of police of the town was there, too, and Monsieur Dumont, the police chief of Bab-El-Kebir, smoking his pipe so hard it was like he was in a oil fire, and he'd hardly speak to me. And the Arabs'd look at Aziza and then at me, and start arguing and hollering so loud it was like shooting crackers going off in your ears.

And a new crowd of Arabs was out in the street, twice as big as the day before, cursing and waving their knives and calling out in French they were going to kill me.

I tell you I know now it's something when you start fooling with a Arab marriage, especially when it's a rich Arab like this trader.

And then the American consul from Algiers came, the same kind of stuffed-shirt fellow that spoke to us when we landed in Africa. He was dressed in the same fancy clothes and talked the same way, like his mouth was full of oatmeal and it was too hot.

"You've put your country in a bad situation, Cullum,"

87

he told me. "Abducting a young girl is a very serious matter anywhere. And it's a frightful crime over here among the Mohammedans. I don't know whether I'll be able to get you out of this or not."

"This wasn't any abduction," I said. "I ain't interested in this girl that way. She's just a kid that worked in my laundry. I ain't a cradle snatcher."

And then I tell him about the speech the other fellow made in the camp.

"He told us we got to show the Arabs that Americans are nice people," I said. "All I was doing was what any American would do when he sees a lady in trouble."

He looked kind of queer and didn't say a word. I guess he knew there wasn't no answer.

Pretty soon I saw Aziza's father and mother take her off to a truck they'd got somewhere and start out for Bab-El-Kebir. And the Consul talked a lot to the police, and I saw him and Monsieur Dumont and all the rest look at me and shake their heads. And finally the Arab crowd in front broke up, and the police let me go, and I took the jeep and drove back to Bab-El-Kebir.

I got to the laundry next day and Louie was looking black as the inside of a Gila monster's stomach. But it seemed like there wasn't anything either he or I could do.

Course, like I expected, Aziza's father and mother didn't let her come back to work in the laundry. I was afraid maybe they'd keep her locked up, but she was smart and come over early one morning and managed to slip over every few days after that for a minute to tell me what's happening.

The pig-eyed man was still around town and I met him

a couple of times going down the street. And each time I saw him I liked him less.

I swore to myself I wasn't going to let him get Aziza, and I talked things over again with her and Miss Peckham, and then I figured out something that it seemed to me couldn't miss. I'd drive Aziza down to the American Army camp near Algiers where I had some married buddies that stayed in the service, and they could take her in for a maid or something. It'd be the easiest thing in the world to get her to Algiers, because that was no distance, and she could be safe with one of my friends long before her parents even knew she was gone.

The chance come quicker than I figured. There was a big Arab holiday like New Year's or something, and all over the oasis you could see men and women all dressed up in new clothes, and kissing each other whenever they met, and drinking coffee and playing drums and dancing. Lots of people come into the oasis, too, and there was a carnival, like they have in the States, with a little Ferris Wheel run by a old Italian and a merry-go-round run by a German and a freak show with a mermaid.

Some of the boys that had been in Bab-El-Kebir when it was a rest camp were on duty in Algiers, and they come down on leave a few days for the fun. A couple of them were going back early the next morning, so when Aziza slipped over that day, I fixed it up with them to take her along. Nobody'd ever look for her in a U.S. Army truck.

I went out with the boys that night taking in the carnival, and then they got the truck ready about daybreak to start off to Algiers. Aziza was supposed to come over while it was still dark. She didn't come though. We waited for

89

a hour or so after the sun was up and there's still no sign of her, so Louie went to see if he could find out what's keeping her, because the boys didn't want to wait too long and be AWOL.

Louie come back in a hurry, and he's gray as the wall of the laundry.

"They're all gone, Joe," he said.

I went with him to her house. It was shut up tight, as if nobody'd been there for years. Wasn't anything there but a couple of lizards running over the sand in front, and a big black bird like a buzzard flying around the roof.

We went out to where they had the tent. It's gone, too, and we could see where the stakes had been pulled up quick.

Louis knocked at the house next door to see if he could find out anything. A woman come out and Louie talked to her a few minutes.

"They left in the middle of the night," he told me when he was finished. "Maybe they heard you were going to try to run off with her again. The pig-eyed man came to the house just after dark with the cadi, and the cadi married them right there. Her mother and father have gone down to the desert with the animals and the money they got, and the pig-eyed man's taken Aziza off to his store in the Rio de Oro with his three other wives. The Arab woman said Aziza was crying so hard when they left the house, she thought at first it was somebody that had been hit by a car in the road."

I felt just like the time when I was a kid and a norther came down when Ma had been working on a ranch a couple of miles from town and she walked all the way back to the house in summer clothes and got pneumonia and the doctor told me she was going to die.

"I'm going out to find her," I said, after I could think a little. "I'll find her if it takes ten years."

Louie shook his head. "You'll never do it, Joe. And even if you did, it wouldn't do any good. She is his wife. Maybe in America it is easy to take away a man's wife. But with an Arab it is easier to take his life."

"I'll find her," I said. "And I'll get her away somehow. I ain't going to let a poor kid like that spend the rest of her life living with a pig."

I went back to the laundry trying to think how I'd get started looking.

Like they say, it never rains but it pours.

I was back of the counter, figuring how maybe I'd hire somebody for a couple of weeks to run the laundry while me and Louie went searching, when in comes Monsieur Dumont with two Arab policemen and a Frenchman I'd never seen before, had a face like a eagle, with eyes that bored right through you. You could tell right away he was a big official.

Before I could even ask what the trouble is, he swung around to the two Arabs.

"Search the place," he snapped, like a eagle biting off your finger.

The two Arabs started turning the laundry upside down, throwing out everything in a big cabinet I had, and poking into baskets for false bottoms, and tearing out the back of the counter, and even ripping out the drain pipes where I got my wash basin.

The eagle-faced man looked at the pile of surplus Army

blankets the Arab had just given me to be cleaned before he sent them down to the desert.

"Now the blankets," he said.

The Arabs piled into them and sliced them up with knives till there wasn't a piece wider than a toothpick hardly. They didn't find nothing, of course, and then the eagle-faced fellow swung around to me.

His eyes burned a couple of holes in my chest.

"Until next time, monsieur," he said, and goes out the door.

Well, the place was a wreck. It looked just like some of the buildings in Black Spring the time the tornado hit. I thought at first it was something Louie had done, but Louie said he didn't know any more than I did.

He went down the street and found out in a few minutes. It was all on account of this Egyptian fellow that had talked to me that was in the black market. He'd got the Arab to come and arrange with me about cleaning the blankets, and then after he picked up the bundles he'd undo them, and put penicillin or guns or anything he wanted between, and then wrap them up again. Nobody'd suspect blankets that just come from a laundry.

With this happening right on top of Aziza going away, I just sat there kind of paralyzed, like I'd been hit in the head by a freight train. But after a while I got hold of myself, and went down with Louie to the square where the carnival is staying to get a drink in the café and try to figure things out again.

It was still morning and the carnival's all quiet, the way they are before business starts for the day. The little Ferris Wheel was on a truck frame towed by a pickup truck right in front of the café, and when I passed by I saw the old Italian trying to fix the engine that made it turn.

He couldn't get it to running, though, and all the while I was having my drink I could see him working. We started back to the laundry and he was still fussing over it, and his shirt was wringing wet with sweat. Like I told you, I'm a good mechanic, working in the Parts Department and everything, and I couldn't see him going on that way, so I stopped and put it in shape for him.

Wasn't anything special I did, but the old Italian thought I was wonderful. We got to talking, and he said he'd been wanting somebody for a long time to help him drive and keep the machinery all right. He said the carnival was breaking up here and he wanted to go on by himself anyway. He said if I came along he'd pay me good, and if I wanted I could take Louie, too. He said he needed a good Arab.

Well, you know how it is sometimes, you make up your mind quicker than a frog that's been out in a Texas drought all summer'll jump into a swimming pool, especially after things happen to you the way they done that morning. Louie said the Italian was going to follow what they call the Trade Route through Tangiers and Morocco that was the same as the pig-eyed man would take with Aziza going back to his store in Rio de Oro. And that way I'd have a good chance of finding her. Traveling in a strange country costs plenty, and I wouldn't get another chance like that in a long time.

Besides, there wasn't any use keeping on with the laundry now, with the place all smashed up and my best customer turning out to be a crook. There wouldn't be any real business left anyway. And this would give me a chance to look around and maybe find a new place to start the business again. Maybe Bab-El-Kebir wasn't the right place for the laundry after all.

And the Italian was offering me good pay and maybe I could save up something and bring Ma over. So it looked like everything made it the right thing to do.

Next morning I stored the laundry machinery in a place where Louie said it'd be safe until we came back, and went around in the jeep to say good-by to Miss Peckham. Her eyes filled with tears when Louie told her he was going away for three or four months or half a year maybe.

She thought a minute and gave him a little Bible, then went to a old trunk and took out a little leather box stamped all in silver and locked with a little silver key.

"This belonged to my father," she said. "He was a sea captain and a holy man. He said this box was his Friend in Need, that he always called on when he was in trouble. I think it contains his favorite passages from the Bible. I give it to you to take on your travels that it may bless you as it blessed Captain Peckham."

Louie put it inside his red coat.

Miss Peckham went out in the kitchen and came back with a box of sandwiches.

"Eat these on the way," she said. "You will be hungry. They are peanut butter and Boston brown bread my friends sent me from Fall River." She tied the box with a piece of faded ribbon. "It will be sad in the Sunday School and the church without you. You have been the jewel the Lord put in my crown and now that only jewel will be gone. I will try not to think of the empty benches."

She walked with us to the door. Her voice got shaky.

"Be back for the anniversary," she said.

We drove down the road. We were in the main part of town, passing one of the cafés when all of a sudden Louie asked me to stop. I put on the brakes and we climbed out. I saw the two Arab bums that he'd brought over to Miss Peckham's sitting at a table.

Louie went up to them and slapped some money down beside their wine glasses.

"You two are going to be Miss Peckham's converts again until I come back," he said. "You be good Christians or I will kill you."

We rode to the square where the old Italian was waiting. I climbed into the pickup truck that pulled the Ferris Wheel and the old man came in beside me. Louie took over the jeep.

We started down the road to Algiers. Crowds of boys ran after us, hollering and asking for pennies, and beggars stood waiting wherever we stopped, motioning for us to put money in their bowls.

We left the town, and picking our way through flocks of sheep and goats, began to climb a yellow mountain.

I turned and looked back. The oasis was laying all spread out under us, with the little houses shining in the sun. I could see the caravans moving out toward the desert, and the flocks of sheep and goats coming into the market, and the Ouleds in the Ouled Square, and the river with the palms and the women washing their clothes, and The Street of the Laughing Camel with all the Arabs walking along it, and the laundry with the sign swinging in the wind.

And I thought of Aziza and Miss Peckham and Ma and the fellow at the Moose and the Army and Black Spring and the Parts Department and all the things that happened to me, and how life was sure funny, you never knew what was coming.

It was kind of like a rodeo. Maybe you'd win the big prize, and then next time a bull would throw you on your head and kill you.

A couple of camels come down ahead of us, carrying some hay.

I swung the Ferris Wheel around them and drove on up the mountain.

CHAPTER TEN

WE STOPPED WITH THE FERRIS WHEEL at some little
towns along the road and then went on to Algiers. Everywhere we went Louie and me kept asking about Aziza.
Now I was really doing something about looking for her
I felt better. And the Italian and me got along fine.

He was a nice old fellow named Gino, with a face all
pock-marked like one of the burned-leather pocketbooks
the Arabs sell you, and he didn't have a plain tooth in his
head. They were all gold, and when he opened his mouth
it shone like when the sun hits the mica hills out in Texas.

He said some people like diamonds to save their money,

97

but he figured gold teeth were better because you couldn't lose them like you could the diamonds.

Italians are nice. And smart, too. They can sure pick out fruit.

From Algiers we went on to Oran and places like that, stopping sometimes two or three days, and sometimes a week. We'd set up the Ferris Wheel in the square, and the Arabs'd come around, and the little Arab girls would climb in and giggle and scream pretending to be scared, just the same as the girls in America. We had a loud-speaker, too, and a old phonograph and some records that played waltzes and things while the Wheel was running.

Like I said, all the time we kept asking about Aziza. The more I thought about it the more it made me feel awful for that poor kid having to live with that kind of man. And I made up my mind I'd find her if I had to follow her all the way to the Rio de Oro.

I'm just built that way, I guess. When I was riding range the ranch boss used to say if I ever got started doing something I'd never quit. If he'd ask me to go out and bring in some poor cow that'd got caught in a blizzard with her calf and got lost, I'd bring them in if I had a arm froze off.

I sure missed Aziza. I didn't know till she was gone how much I liked having her around.

Gino and me were doing all right, and I guess we'd have stayed together a long time, but we crossed over into Spanish Morocco and got to Tangiers and Gino ate some meat that wasn't good. Course you can't get Western beef in Tangiers. And he got pretty sick. A Italian fellow he knowed and his wife took him over to their house and Louie and me ran the Wheel.

He stayed sick for longer than he figured and he looked terrible shaky. And late one night, after the Wheel closed and I come over to the house to talk to him like I always did, I could see he had something on his mind.

"I not feel so good, Joe," he said. "I think maybe not a good thing I go on the road no more. My friend Alberto, owns this house, he wish to start a pizza restaurant and he asks me to be partners. She is the big thing now, the pizza. And I have told Alberto I will do it. Do you wish to buy the Wheel, Joe? I will sell him. Very cheap."

Well, I had a few hundred dollars in back pay I'd just got a couple of weeks before, and course I told you I always liked to have my own business, that's the way you make a big success. And having the Wheel myself, if I felt like going someplace where I figured Aziza might be, I could do it in a way I couldn't when it belonged to Gino. So I said all right.

I had the Wheel in Tangiers a week maybe. We kept it down in the square near the docks, and one afternoon a American sailor, what they call a bosun's mate, that was off a Navy ship in the harbor, came up and we began talking.

He told me he'd been a big fellow in show business before he joined the Navy, and he found out I'd been a cowboy and he said I ought to fix up cowboy costumes for me and Louie and stand out in front and twirl lassoos and do tricks with a rope. He said the Arabs were crazy about cowboys.

You don't meet a smart fellow knows about show business like that every day. So I got a Arab tailor to fix us up a couple of cowboy suits out of old Army uniforms. The Arab didn't need any telling how a cowboy looked, he'd

99

seen so many in the movies. And I got a couple of hill-billy records to play on the phonograph.

Well, about now we heard that a fellow who sounded like the pig-eyed man had passed that way a while ago and had gone over into what they call Spanish Morocco. That was right on the way to Rio de Oro, so we went, too.

We drove on a little way and pretty soon we came to a little town had a mosque with a tower made of tiles so red it looked like it was on fire. The whole town was covered with red dust, so thick you could take one of the big lizards that were around and bury him in the dust anywhere.

We set up the Wheel near the market and Louie and me put on the cowboy suits. Louie with his little monkey body sure looked funny wearing chaps and spurs and a big Army hat.

I took a rope and began showing him how to throw a lassoo. But I guess it ain't easy unless you're born to it. His pants weren't cut right and they were always sliding down someway. When he tried to lassoo a goat or a donkey that was passing you'd have swore he was one of them cowboy clowns in a rodeo that stand by a barrel waiting to jump in when the bull comes charging at him.

The Arabs sure liked us. Everybody in the place came, pretty near. Like the Navy fellow told me, they were crazy about cowboys.

"Looks like the Wheel's going to do fine here in Morocco," I said. "We've sure got something now. And we've struck a fine town. The way people are piling up we're going to make plenty. If we could just find Aziza everything'd be wonderful."

We hadn't been there long when I seen a nice-dressed,

kind of rich-looking old man with a cane studying the Wheel and watching me twirl the rope, and then he finally come over.

He told me he was a Dutchman that was retired and the only European man living in this town where he'd been for forty years. I guess he was kind of lonely.

We talked for a while—he spoke English all right—and then he got ready to go. He was a fine old man, but he was sure gloomy.

"I ought to warn you, my friend," he said. "This can be a dangerous country. These Moroccans are very suspicious and very touchy. It is easy for a stranger like yourself with this Wheel to get into serious difficulty. The farther you go the more dangerous it will become. It might even cost your life. I advise you to be very careful."

He went off and I got busy with the Wheel again.

There were some other little shows in the square, some dancers that had bells on their feet, and a storyteller with a fellow playing the bagpipes, and a snake charmer had a couple of big cobras. They were doing a good business till we got there, but then all the Arabs came over to the Wheel and they didn't have nobody.

A little while after the Dutchman spoke to me I noticed the dancers and the snake charmer and the others talking and staring at us and looking mad, but I didn't pay too much attention.

We kept the Wheel running till midnight, pretty near. And the Arabs were waiting in a line three deep. But there wasn't anybody went to the other shows at all.

I sure felt sorry for those other fellows.

We closed up and Louie said he figured we ought to stay there a week anyway. And then we went over to the little hotel where we were stopping, and Louie fell into his bed because he'd been working awful hard, and in about a minute was asleep. I finished brushing my teeth and turned out the light and crawled in my bed, pretty tired and sleepy, too. My arm was all wore out from throwing so many lassoos. And then all of a sudden my foot touched something cold and slimy under the covers.

Well, in those hot countries when you feel something that ain't right it's a good idea to get away from it, and I slid out of bed as easy as I could and clicked on the light. And then I threw back the bedcovers.

And there was a big cobra, sitting up with his hood spread out, and his long tongue darting like a fork of lightning.

I'm used to rattlers—I killed plenty out in Texas—but I never seen anything as wicked-looking as that snake in my life. He looked just like the Devil, waving a pitchfork.

I called to Louie quiet to wake up, because Louie's bed was awful close to mine and he was one of those fellows that always tossed around a lot while he slept. I didn't want the snake striking at his leg or arm maybe if he swung around that way.

But Louie was too tired, I guess, and he kind of grunted, and went on sleeping like he was before.

I slipped over easy to my suitcase where I had my pistol, keeping a eye on the cobra all the time, because I'd heard they'll charge you sometimes if they're mad. I went all through that suitcase trying to do everything awful quiet so the snake wouldn't get more excited. But I couldn't find the gun anywhere. And all the while the snake just stayed with that forked tongue dancing and his little beady eyes watching me every second. And then I remembered the pistol wasn't in the suitcase after all. I'd left it out in the jeep.

I called to Louie low again, because he's starting to throw himself around with a bad dream or something. And this time he hears me and jerks up in bed. I guess he must have scared the cobra because it swung around and hit at him quicker than a bullet. But Louie jumped just in time and the cobra missed him by what looked to me no more than a horsehair.

Louie was out of that bed faster than I ever saw a human move before. He picked up a chair there by him and hit at the snake's head. But he missed and the snake gave another strike at him, but 'way off this time. And then it whipped across the room, and went down through a hole in the floor.

Right then I had a feeling somebody was at the door looking in, and I ran to it and jerked it open, just in time to see the snake charmer running in his bare feet along the hall. A minute later he went out of sight down the stairs.

Louie was looking pretty white. The sweat was running down his face like somebody'd splashed him with a bucket of water.

"We'd better get out of here fast, Joe," he said. "Before they send the cobra's sister."

We threw on our clothes and hurried out to the cars and started driving, and we didn't stop till we came to the next town, fifty miles away.

Next morning we were eating breakfast in a café when

Louie starts talking about the snake. He took out the little leather box Miss Peckham gave him and looked at it a minute kind of thoughtful.

"I was lucky when the cobra struck at me, Joe," he said. "Maybe this holy charm that was good for Miss Peckham's father is good for me also. She said this holy charm had a name. But I do not remember. I would like to know the name of this holy charm that saved my life."

"She said her father that was a sea captain called it the Friend in Need," I answered. "It helped him whenever he was in trouble. She said she thought it had his favorite verses from the Bible."

Louie studied it a long time, then took the little key tied by a silver chain to the top.

"I think I will open it, Joe," he said.

He put the key in the lock and lifted the cover.

Inside was a pack of playing cards and a pair of dice.

Well, we went on for a few days, and we heard about what sounded like the pig-eyed man ahead of us again, but then we lost track.

Louie was kind of discouraged. He was feeling blue about being away from his own country, and he began talking about what the Dutchman told us, how maybe it was too dangerous, and maybe we ought to sell the Wheel and go back to Algeria and do something else before a worse thing than the cobra happened to us. He said he could make a good living for us picking pockets in Algiers where we wouldn't get into no trouble.

But I said I wasn't going to stop till I found Aziza, even if I had to go to the Rio de Oro by myself. And after I done a lot of arguing he seen I was right.

We went on to a lot of other towns. Casablanca, that's

a good place, had a lot of Americans, and then we come to a big town named Marrakeesh, had a big square that was just like Ringling Brothers Circus. There were black men up from the Congo playing on big drums, and men who ate fire like it was cotton candy, and religious fellows running around in circles, hitting their elbows against their sides and hollering like coyotes, and men telling fortunes with sand, and a donkey that drank tea out of a saucer like a person, and jugglers and acrobats that kept spinning like pinwheels on the Fourth of July.

All around were camels and donkeys and sheep and goats and people selling meat and vegetables and witch doctors with charms that if you didn't like somebody would dry them up till they were a skeleton. It looked like the State Fair in Texas.

We set up the Wheel and put on the cowboy suits and we did a good business. There was a lot of them Foreign Legion fellows in Marrakeesh. You could see them around all the time, collecting garbage and things like that. It wasn't like what you see in the movies. And they spent plenty of money bringing their girls down to give them a ride.

Well, Louie kind of thought the pig-eyed man might be in Marrakeesh buying things because it was a big trading place, so all the time I kept watching out for Aziza. And one day I was walking by myself over to the hotel, wondering if maybe she was here, when I saw a young Arab girl with a fat Arab woman buying meat at a butcher stand.

Course both of them were veiled. But something about the girl made me look at her again. She had little hands and feet, and a pretty little body the same as Aziza. And then I saw her big brown eyes, and I'm sure it's her.

I pretty near jumped out of my skin.

I hurried up to her and I saw her give me a funny look, and then the fat woman grabbed her by the hand and pulled her around to the other side of the meat stand and started running. I ran after them. But it was awful crowded with all the camels and goats and people, and everything got in my way.

I managed to keep close behind them, though, and I ran after them into what they call the *souks*. They're places covered by awnings, with all kinds of booths for selling perfume and cushions and jewelry and clothes, going on for miles and miles. The *souks* were as crowded as the square outside, and every ten feet I'd come to a new covered street going off every which way. It was just like what they call the Mystic Maze they have in a Fun House in a carnival.

I was almost up with Aziza and I thought next minute I'd be able to catch hold of her and grab her away from the fat woman, when a camel came out of a doorway in front of me and the street was so narrow he had it blocked. And when he moved off and I could get by, they were gone.

I looked all over, but the more I looked the more mixed up I got. I went back to the Wheel where Louie was running things, and we closed it for a while, and Louie and me came to the place where I'd left them and started to look again. But after a while Louie stopped.

"We will never find her this way, Joe," he said. "You could search in these *souks* for fifty years and they could have an elephant and it would still be hidden. I will ask some of the thieves in the market if they have seen this merchant. He is rich and if he is here, maybe the thieves will know."

He asked everybody but he couldn't find out anything. I figured it didn't really mean the pig-eyed man wasn't there, though, because Marrakeesh is a big town, kind of like New York to the Arabs, I guess, and I knew the girl I seen was Aziza.

Sure enough, I was in the square a couple of nights later and I seen her again, walking with the fat woman. They didn't see me because it was pretty dark, and this time I figured I'd be careful. I followed behind them when they went into the *souks*, and they kept twisting and turning down all kinds of streets until they came to the door of a Arab house. And the fat woman knocked. And a servant opened the door and the Arab girl started going through.

I ran forward, ready to do something, I don't know what, maybe run into the house after her.

"Aziza!" I called.

She turned around fast, being surprised that way. But I didn't get a chance to say anything more. The fat woman jerked her inside, and then a big Arab servant came out, and he started chasing me, hollering in Arab. And a bunch of other fellows that were in the street started running after me, too.

Lucky for me it was awful dark, and in those narrow places twisting every which way I lost them pretty quick. But I sure was lost, too. I wandered around in that pitch black for three or four hours, I guess, expecting every minute to see a knife coming at me out of some doorway. And then I seen lights and it was the market place, and I was all right.

I kept on looking with Louie all over Marrakeesh after that, trying to find the house again, but all the places were exactly alike. I couldn't get no trace.

We stayed on in Marrakeesh, doing good business. About this time I seen the Arabs buying a kind of soda water they called Orange Drink a American company was just starting in Morocco. Like I told you, the Arabs ain't allowed to drink liquor, so they liked them soft drinks fine. And I figured it'd be a good thing to get the Orange Drink for the Wheel.

I talked to the Frenchman that was handling it there. He told me a big American company named Trans-Africa Enterprises owned it. They sold all kinds of things all over Africa.

I took a couple of cases and the Arabs bought them right away. And then Louie got a Arab to make a little stand we could carry in the pickup, and those bottles went so fast it looked like we had to get a new supply every minute.

We were in Marrakeesh a month, maybe. And one afternoon a sergeant in the Air Force that had a base there come up and we got to talking about Army camps and things, and he was complaining about how awful the place was where they had his camp. He said he figured before they put a new camp anywhere the big generals 'd meet and they'd take a map and say "Where's the worst swamp in this country?" or "Where's the worst desert?" and they'd go out and find it and that's where they'd put the camp. And I said he was sure right.

And then we got to talking about the Wheel and the Orange Drink. And he told me that just a couple of weeks ago he and some of his outfit had been up in the Atlas Mountains that we could see from Marrakeesh, all red and white with snow on them, like a strawberry sundae, and he said he bet there'd never been anything like the Ferris Wheel up there, and he bet we could make a lot of money with the Wheel and the drink.

I was pretty interested, and then a pickpocket Louie was talking to said he'd seen a trader that seemed just like the pig-eyed man a week before. The pickpocket had gone through this fellow's clothes in the market and told Louie he was plenty rich. And he had a wife looked just like Aziza. The pickpocket said he'd heard this pig-eyed man say he had to do some trading up in the mountains on his way to his store down in the South. It sure sounded like the man we were after because this way across the Atlas was one of the main routes to the Rio de Oro, and we knew he'd have to be heading there with Aziza anyhow. So right off I decided to go.

Some of the French people told me like the Dutch fellow that it was awful risky. They said the Arabs up there were the wildest Arabs of all, and they didn't want anybody wasn't a Arab coming around. They said the mountains never had been what they call pacified. The soldiers and the police never went anywhere by themselves, because the Arabs had killed plenty of them, and plenty of people like me.

Louie made a bad fuss about going again, but in a couple of days we were all ready to start out.

Just as we were leaving I saw some fireworks in a French store they were selling cheap, and I figured they'd be nice to draw a crowd, especially at night. So I went in and bought a lot of them, skyrockets and Roman candles and things like that. And we piled them in the back of the pickup and drove off.

I thought I'd seen the Atlas Mountains when I went to Bab-El-Kebir. But they were like the little piles of earth outside a prairie dog hole compared to these mountains in Morocco. Cliffs straight down so far a camel caravan at the bottom looked like ants, and the road was so steep and narrow a snake'd have to back up a couple of times to get around a curve.

I tell you handling that Wheel was something, specially when the wind was blowing. And it was sure a lonely country. You'd go for hours and not see anything. Just red rocks and maybe a hyena crossing the road, or a eagle flying, or a snake big enough to swallow a cow.

But it was worth it when you got to one of the towns. They were all one building, kind of skyscrapers like New York, only course these were only seven or eight stories, built close to the side of a mountain. I guess they were some of the first skyscrapers in the world.

Outside they looked like the biggest fort you ever saw, with towers and narrow little windows in the walls they could shoot at you through. And then you went past a big wooden gate they could shut if anybody came to attack, and there was a big court with kind of a little town inside, meat and vegetable stands and little stores, and then above that the rooms in the skyscraper where all the people lived.

We stopped at one of the biggest skyscrapers and tied some of the Roman candles and skyrockets to the Wheel and lighted the fuse we'd fixed and started the Wheel turning to get a crowd coming. It was sure pretty with them all going off. They looked just like the pinwheels we used to have back home on the Fourth of July. Like the Air Force fellow said, the people there had never seen a Wheel before, and they all wanted to have a ride. A lot of them were wild-looking, big long-haired fellows carrying a couple of knives in their belts. You'd think they'd cut your throat for a nickel.

There were some Foreign Legion fellows there, too. Funny, a lot of the Legion soldiers was German, and you'd hear them talking German so much sometimes I'd think I was back at the prison camp near Algiers where I went once during the war.

Generally I got along with the Legionnaires fine, but some of these fellows around the skyscraper had been drinking bad, and when they got their girls up in the Wheel, they started fooling and told the girls they were in a airplane that was going to make a crash landing. And they began pulling off bolts and things from the seats, so they'd come loose and give the girls a little scare.

Course, I didn't want anybody to get hurt and I made them stop, and some of them got kind of sore.

A couple of hours later me and Louie were eating supper in the French café when a bunch of the Legionnaires come in, drunker than ever, and I could see they're looking for a fight. There was one big blond fellow, a Czech or something, spoke English, that was one of those I stopped from bothering the Wheel, and he saw me and came up to the table, and started talking tough.

"The Ferris Wheel stinks," he said.

I didn't pay any attention.

"Orange Drink stinks," he said this time.

I got a little mad. "Don't annoy me, garbage collector,"

I said, meaning the way I saw them collecting garbage.

Louie touched me on the arm. "Take it easy, Joe," he said. "Orange Drink isn't the American flag."

The blond fellow came closer and leaned over me like a big yellow bear. "You stink," he said. "Everything in America stinks."

Course that was too much. And in a second I was up from the table, and there was a big battle with everybody in the café joining in.

And then the Frenchman that owned the place blew a whistle, and before you know it me and the blond fellow were in jail.

CHAPTER ELEVEN

I̲ᴛ ᴡᴀs ᴀ ᴍɪʟɪᴛᴀʀʏ ᴊᴀɪʟ, because this skyscraper village
was run by the Army people.

I felt awful bad that I couldn't get out to hunt for
Aziza. But Louie told me he'd be on the lookout every
minute. And he said maybe it was all right, because sometimes you could find out about things like that quicker in
a jail than anywhere else.

We were high up, and out the window I could see what
they call terraces made of mud and rocks where the people
were working in little fields and gardens, and then in back
were the mountains. And on some of them you could see
other skyscrapers, too.

There was just a few prisoners. There were some Legionnaires, and a Spanish fellow was in for counterfeiting money, and a gypsy they said had stole a horse, and a Belgian that was in the black market. There was a Bulgarian or something, too, a dark kind of man stayed off by himself all the time, never spoke to anybody. I heard they were holding him to send back to France for a spy.

I never thought it'd be that way but that jail in Africa was kind of a education for a fellow like me never went past the fifth grade. A fellow could learn more about the world there in a day than he could at Black Spring in a year.

We all stayed in one big room except the Bulgarian, and he was in a special place a little off to the side.

Sometimes the Spanish fellow'd tell us all about Spain and the bullfights. He'd started out being a bullfighter when he was young, he said, and it looked like he was going to be the best bullfighter in Spain. And then he was in the ring one afternoon fighting a terrible black bull when all of a sudden he sees the bull's head change to a skull and crossbones. And he knows that's a sign if he keeps on fighting the bull he's going to die. So he throws down his sword and walks out of the ring, and everybody starts hollering and spitting at him. And he can't do any more bullfighting, so he takes up counterfeiting.

The gypsy—he was from France—told us interesting things, too. How if you were hungry and wanted a chicken you took a fishhook tied to a string and put a piece of bread on it, and threw the hook over into a chicken yard. And when the chicken grabbed the bread you pulled him up, and you had plenty of white meat for supper.

I was sleeping right next to the blond fellow I got in the

114

fight with in the café. And when you got to know him he was all right.

Seems he wasn't a Czech, he was a Swede. His father owned a big brewery in Stockholm, he said, and he went in the Legion when a rich society girl there run off with another fellow the day before they were going to be married. He'd forgot all about the girl now and was getting out of the Legion in six months and going back to Sweden to take over the brewery.

He said he wanted a American representative for his beer—he said Swedish beer was the best in the world because they had that wonderful cold water from them icebergs—and he said if I wanted to he'd give me the job. He seen I was a good business man, he said.

I told him I figured on staying in Africa for a while, but if I decided to leave I'd sure come in with him.

Funny, ain't it, how you'd get a offer of a wonderful job like that in a jail.

Course Louie came to see me every morning and told me if there was any news about Aziza and how the Wheel was doing, and after ten days they let me go, and we started out again.

Well, the way Louie heard, the fellow that seemed like he was the pig-eyed man kept heading South through the Atlas toward the Rio de Oro. So we figured more and more that it was him, and went the same way.

We got along fine with the Wheel. You wouldn't think there were so many people in those skyscrapers. They came out just like the time in Texas when I was riding fences and a tractor hit a old cottonwood trunk maybe fifteen feet high, and the ants ran out by the millions, all the way from the bottom to the top.

We didn't use the fireworks except when we came to a big place, because we didn't have too many and we wanted to make them last as long as they could.

After a while we crossed the mountains, and come down in the desert on the other side. It was the wildest country I ever seen. We were right out in the Sahara. Nothing but big dunes that looked like waves, and stretching so far out you felt like you were crossing the ocean. And the sand was blowing all the time till on top of some of the big dunes you could see sand rainbows. A dozen times a day the jeep or the Wheel would get stuck and we'd have to take shovels and dig out.

There were a lot of caravans going through with all kinds of people, sometimes the black Hausa traders and the Arabs coming up from the South on their way to Mecca, that's the Arab holy place. And sometimes the camels would have fancy seats on their backs made of wood, like you see on elephants in the circus, where some big Arab would be riding, with a kind of tent over his head to keep off the hot sun.

We were on what they call the Slave Route now. Course, slavery was terribly against the law, but just the same there was plenty of it. They brought up black slaves from the Congo or poor Arabs that couldn't pay their debts, maybe a whole family, and sent them over to the rich Arabs in Arabia.

The people around in the desert were mostly the Blue Arabs—their name's the Tuaregs a fellow told me—with their faces painted all blue just like you painted a house. And funny thing about those Blue Arabs, it was the men that wore the veils. And there were a lot of what they call the Black Arabs, too. They're colored people, but they don't look like the colored people we got back home. Some of them have beards like that little king from Ethiopia I seen in the movies.

We were crossing some dunes looked pretty near like mountains, when we stopped at a well under some palm trees to eat. There were some caravans letting their camels drink and Louie heard from a Arab traveling with them about a big oasis a little way off that was a good trading place where the pig-eyed man would be pretty sure to go and that ought to be a good place for the Wheel. So we figured we'd drive there.

We were still under the palms eating, when a Legion patrol come up and stopped near us to rest a few minutes. I got to talking to one of the officers and told him about the oasis we were starting out for.

He shook his head. "I would not visit this place if I were you, monsieur," he said. "It is not safe for anyone except an Arab to go among these people. They are religious fanatics, a sect called the Aisawa. They have processions where they beat themselves with whips and chains, and in a few hours they are crazy. They will be having the processions now. If you go there with this Wheel I am afraid a serious accident will happen."

The Legion fellows left and we had coffee, and I decided we'd go anyhow. Like I said, you can't pay too much attention to the way people talk or you'd never do anything. We arrived at the oasis next morning and set up the Wheel in the market like we always done.

It was a big oasis like we'd heard, crowded with camels and the Blue Arabs with the veils and some of the Black Arabs with the beards. A little way off I could see some other Arabs playing big drums.

Louie said we'd better take it easy and not light the fireworks or anything, till we saw how things were going, because maybe we wouldn't want to stay. But we started the loudspeaker playing a hillbilly record, and Louie and me began throwing lassoos and doing the rope tricks. A bunch of Arabs came around, but they weren't smiling like they did most times, they just stood there looking fierce.

I could see right off they didn't like us, and pretty soon the big drums began to boom louder, and a lot of the Arabs near us threw off the sheets they were wearing so they had nothing on but a piece of burlap around their waists.

And then each of them picked up a chain, like tire chains, from a pile. And they began going around and around in a circle, beating each other with the chains, each man hitting the fellow in front of him on the naked back till the blood came.

They stopped the circling after a while and some flutes began to play wild music. And the Arabs started bending over and roaring like lions and pretty soon they're all foaming at the mouth. And then they began eating live scorpions and chewing glass and swallowing nails and sticking knives in their arms and bodies and beating themselves with the chains again.

A old Arab with a kind of rusty beard that reached pretty near to his waist was standing by them. I guess he was the priest or the mayor or something.

The music got wilder and some of the Arabs began pulling down big batches of prickly-pear cactus that was growing everywhere. And they dropped the cactus on the ground till it was like a carpet, and then they threw themselves on it pretty near naked, so that hundreds of the cactus stickers went in their bodies. After that a fellow run around burning himself with hot irons, and then another put big ship's chains across his shoulders and broke them with his muscles like they were made of candy.

And the music got so loud and crazy, and the fellows got to jumping and hollering so, it was like a lunatic asylum when everybody had broke loose.

And then they stopped, and the ceremony was over and I thought maybe we'd do some business now. But they didn't come for a ride at all. Instead they just crowded around the Wheel, and looked at it fiercer and fiercer.

I got kind of worried and I turned off the loudspeaker, thinking maybe that's what was bothering them. But they still kept on glaring.

"I think they're getting ready for trouble, Joe," Louie said. "These Aisawa aren't like the Arabs in Bab-El-Kebir. We should have listened to the Legionnaire."

All of a sudden the crowd in front kind of broke apart, and a giant of a fellow with a twisted face that looked like somebody you see in a nightmare started running toward us with a club. And all the other Arabs were right behind.

They came charging toward the Wheel to break it up with their bare hands, I guess.

I pulled out my pistol and they drew back a little way. And then some of them run up to the booths in the market and grabbed the oily rags the people used for torches at night. And then the men run back and lit the rags and got ready to throw them at the Wheel to set it on fire.

The old Arab with the beard had come up with the

others, but he wasn't holding a rag or anything. He hadn't done any of the chain beating or glass eating, either. All the time he'd just waited there quiet.

Now he was standing near the Wheel, like a captain with his company in a army, while the crazy fellows stayed in a kind of line, watching him and waiting for him to tell them what to do.

Louie and me was watching him, too, the way you watch a rattler when he's getting ready to strike.

All of a sudden I see Louie hurry up to him and start talking very soft and soothing. And the old man burst out like he was exploding, with his rusty beard jerking up and down like when you were tossing hay.

And then he stood quiet again like he was one of the rocks you could see out in the desert.

I kept my pistol showing and moved up to Louie.

"What's the matter?" I asked kind of under my breath.

"They've never seen anything like the Wheel before," Louie answered. "They saw all the radar machines and the tanks and bazookas in the war that killed people. They think this is some new kind of war machine. And they want to burn it up before it kills them all. I've told the old man it's just for pleasure. But I can't tell what he's going to do."

Just then one of the Arabs threw a burning rag toward the truck. It landed on the floor at the back, and in a minute it would have had the truck blazing.

I slapped out the flames with a board laying there, and then a couple more fellows threw rags and I put them out, too.

We stood again for a couple of minutes with nobody

120

moving a muscle. I felt the way I guess a sheep does, watching a bunch of coyotes closing in.

I could see Louie was thinking hard.

"If we could get this old man to take a ride maybe we'd be out of trouble," he said. "Climb in one of the cars, Joe."

I got in like he said and Louie switched on the loudspeaker and started the Wheel to turning slow.

The old man got all kinds of funny expressions on his face, then began watching the Wheel like he was hypnotized.

While I was riding a fellow in the crowd threw a burning rag that landed in a car near me, but it went out right away.

After the Wheel had been running a couple of minutes, I hopped out and Louie went over to the old man and began talking to him again.

The old Arab kind of hesitated, then stepped into the car waiting at the bottom. He sat stiff as a statue while the Wheel kept circling, looking like a preacher at a funeral.

And then all of a sudden there was a terrible explosion. I thought for a minute somebody had throwed a hand grenade or a bomb maybe. But it was the fireworks tied to the Wheel. The rag the last fellow threw must have kept on kind of smoldering and one of the sparks set fire to a fuse. In a second Roman candles and skyrockets were going off till it looked like D-Day on the beach in North Africa.

Some camels and donkeys were standing there, and they run in every direction across the market place, like they were burning instead of the fireworks. And the people were worse than the animals, knocking over meat and date stands, and spilling everything on the ground, they were trying so hard to get away. I guess they'd never seen any fireworks. And all the time the Wheel was going round and round, with the old man holding onto his seat, white as ashes, while the rockets and Roman candles were exploding all around him and he was giving a jump like a jack rabbit each time a new one went off.

I rushed up as soon as I could and shut off the motor. And pretty soon the Wheel stopped and the fireworks died down.

The people all came running back now, looking wild, wanting to rescue their boss and ready to tear us to pieces.

The old Arab stepped out of the car with his face and body all stony, like somebody walking in his sleep.

And I got my pistol ready to fight for our lives, because I figured after what had happened we were done for.

All of a sudden the old man's face broke into a big smile that showed all his white teeth. He turned to Louie and pointed to some of the dead fireworks laying on the ground and then looked off at the Wheel.

"Like the stars and the moon," he said.

And then all the rest of the people saw him smiling so they smiled, too.

We gave the old Arab and some of the others a few of the Roman candles, and showed them how to light the fuses, to keep them feeling good. It about used up all our fireworks, but we figured it was sure worth the price. They started kind of shooting the candles at each other. And we got away from there as quick as the time I saw a tornado coming when I was driving a herd across the Concho River out in Texas.

A couple of days later we heard about the pig-eyed man having come through ahead of us again, and we kept on going through the big dunes. Except for getting stuck in the sand all the time, things were pretty quiet for a while. We passed more caravans, and maybe on some of the camels you'd see a old woman riding or a baby camel that had just been born tucked in a saddlebag. And you'd know that one of them was too old and one was too young to walk.

And sometimes when it got dark we'd camp out in the desert where they'd stopped. And we'd finish our supper and I'd watch the Arabs sleeping in the sand by their camels and maybe a Arab sitting by the fire keeping watch against robbers. And I'd think how it was like the Parts Department. The Arabs and the camels sure fitted living in this desert, just like the hub caps and the spark plugs and the fuses fitted in the little spaces you had for them in the wall.

And then one afternoon we came to a pretty little oasis that was kind of like Bab-El-Kebir. There were a lot of palm trees and yellow houses and women washing clothes in a little river. It was still the Blue Arab country and the Blue Arabs looked wonderful riding their white horses.

We were on the Slave Route again and we were hearing about the traders taking slaves through all the time now. That night after we shut up the Wheel we were passing a high wall in front of a Arab house when I saw Louie stop fast.

He went close to the wall and listened.

"It's slaves," he said.

I could kind of hear people talking in low voices. But it was Arab and course I didn't know what they're saying.

Louie moved up closer, then went around the corner of the street where there was a big wooden gate, and we looked through a crack. We could see plain as day in the moonlight. There was a Arab man and a woman, and four beautiful little girls; one of them about sixteen kind of reminded me of Aziza. It made me go all cold to see her. One of the girls was maybe thirteen, and the others ten and eight maybe.

They didn't have chains on like I figured slaves would have. And there didn't seem to be anybody watching them. But I guess they didn't need anything, because that wall was so high nobody could ever have climbed over, and the door was heavy planks a couple of inches thick with a lock on it big as the locks in a bank.

"They're from down in the desert," Louie said, after he listened to them talk awhile. "The father got in trouble borrowing money some way from a rich Arab and a trader's taking them to sell as slaves in Arabia for the debt."

Course, I'd heard about slaves people used to have down South, but that was finished a long time ago. I sure never expected to see slaves in my own life. The father and the mother were awful sad, just sat there bent over looking at the ground, and the two oldest girls were crying all the time, like their hearts would break.

It made me feel terrible. I stood there watching I don't know how long, and then I turned to Louie.

"We got to let them out," I said.

Louie got awful nervous.

"Don't you do it, Joe," he said. "The slave traders'll kill you if you let these girls get away."

I didn't pay any attention.

I had a good kit of tools in the jeep, so I went back and

got them. And course once I got started Louie helped fine.

Louie figured the traders were in the house back of where the slaves were, and we worked awful quiet with the hacksaw, so if anybody was staying up to keep guard they wouldn't hear anything. We worked fast and we had that lock sawed off in no time. And then we took a good look through the crack again to make sure there wasn't a Arab off in the shadows somewhere, and then we opened the gate easy so it wouldn't creak, and slipped inside.

The people were awful scared when they saw me and Louie come through the entrance. They jumped like rabbits. And I guess they'd have made a lot of noise, except Louie signaled them to keep quiet. The father didn't want to go at first when Louie told him we'd come to set them free. He thought it was a trick, I guess, maybe figuring we were going to steal them and sell them somewhere else. But pretty soon he realized it was the truth. And you never saw a look like the one that come into his face.

We got everybody out of the place without making a sound. And then we took them all over to the Wheel, and gave them a good meal. I could see they hadn't had anything to eat hardly, and we always had a lot of canned things handy for the times we had to camp out. And then we went with them to the Army place that was like the police station so the Arabs would be scared to make them slaves again, because it was terrible against the law. So then we figured they'd be safe.

Well, they stayed by the Wheel that night and we stayed right with them. They were nice people, and the man and the girls could talk a little French, and all they did was thank me.

And I was wishing the American Consul that spoke to us when we landed about the way Americans ought to act had been along, because this time I sure did what he said.

In the morning the father told us they had cousins or something in a town close by—all them Arab people's related, looks like—so we drove them over. The cousins were poor people, even poorer than Aziza. Wasn't nothing in the house but a little Arab table and some mattresses made of straw.

The mother of the family we'd got away from the slave trader said they all wanted to give me a big dinner next day, to show me how grateful they were for setting them free. I didn't like them to do it, but I could see they wanted to bad. So me and Louie went.

We sat down cross-legged at the Arab table with the father and the four girls, and the mother waited on us. The girls were pretty little things, like I said, and they talked and smiled all the time.

And they gave us something made of tomatoes and eggs all hot with peppers, and the cous-cous they ate all the time. That's ground-up meal looks like you're digging into a ant hill. But the girls kept talking about the big surprise that was coming.

I thought maybe it was a roast lamb, because that's what the Arabs have for something special, and I asked them but they said no. And finally they all looked at their mother and she comes out of the kitchen with the surprise.

It's a American can of pressed meat, you know that awful stuff made of all the scraps they sweep up off the floor in a packing plant at the end of the day and squeeze it up and put in a can and send it off to the Army, so the Army cooks can give it to you three times a day. That way it'd keep you sick all the time and you wouldn't have no appetite and the cooks wouldn't have to do no work.

Someway this Arab family'd heard from one of their relatives who had been around the Army camps that they always gave American soldiers this pressed meat and they figured it was the Americans' favorite dish.

If there's one thing I never wanted to see again after I got out of the Army, it was a can of pressed meat. But I knew they must have had a awful time getting it. Maybe they begged it or something from the French Army because the French had a lot of American things. So when they sliced it up and put it on the table I pretended I liked it better than anything I ever ate in my life. I didn't leave a scrap, even if it did pretty near choke me to death.

It got late and we told them good-by and went on to the next oasis not far away, and drove to the hotel and went to sleep. And I woke up and went out to the sidewalk café to have breakfast with Louie, and who was there but one of the little girls that we'd let go free, the ten-year-old one, looking very stiff and solemn.

"What's she doing here?" I asked Louie.

He talked to her a minute and I saw his face go kind of funny.

"Her parents say the can of meat wasn't enough," he told me. "They've sent her to you as a present. For your wife."

I guess if a grasshopper'd have brushed against me, I'd have fallen over, the way they say.

I turned to Louie in a hurry.

"You tell her she's got to go right back," I said. "You take the jeep and drive her over to her people right now."

Louie talked to her again.

"She says she can't go home," he told me. "She says her parents went away with her cousins last night to be sure the Arab wouldn't catch them again. She doesn't know where they have gone."

CHAPTER TWELVE

Wᴇʟʟ, ᴛʜᴇʀᴇ ᴡᴀsɴ'ᴛ ᴀɴʏᴛʜɪɴɢ but to take her with us till we figured out what to do. We couldn't leave her in the desert by herself.

She sure looked cute, with coal-black hair and kind of green eyes, and wearing a little yellow Arab robe with a yellow turban and a red belt and red shoes. They'd fixed her up fine.

She just stood there looking at me mighty thoughtful—I seen right away she was a serious little girl—and I made her sit down between us and have breakfast.

There was a store next door that had French things in it, and I bought her a couple of dolls as big as she was, pretty near. She looked like a doll herself.

I bought her a rubber ball and some jacks, too, and a

skipping rope and a game they call Parchesi I used to play in Black Spring. And she took the rope and skipped with it, very solemn, all the way around the square.

She played all day with the dolls and the jacks and the other things. And then she took a ride in the Ferris Wheel, and she sat there in her yellow robe like a little queen.

And then it started getting dark, and I took her back to the hotel, and all of a sudden she turned to me.

"Where is the kitchen?" she said. "I am your wife. My mother told me to cook your meals for you."

"We eat in a restaurant," I told her.

She shook her head. "My mother told me I must cook your meals for you," she said.

She was a stubborn little piece. And she made me take her back to the Wheel where Louie was, and made him go out with her while she bought some vegetables and a couple of little clay pots and some charcoal. And then she fixed us a meal.

It was all right, too. Louie said the Arab girls learned to cook soon as they could talk pretty near. She said her name was Zuleima.

I got a little extra room for her so she could go to bed, but when Louie and me came back she was waiting up for us, playing with her dolls. And then she saw that a pair of my pants and a robe of Louie's had torn places in them.

"I will sew them for you," she said.

And she put away the dolls and took a needle out of the little bundle of clothes she brought with her, and had the holes fixed in a jiffy. And then I saw her head nodding and I made her go to sleep.

I tell you that little Zuleima was a card. We couldn't

leave anything around had a worn place that she wouldn't mend it right away. And she washed our cowboy suits, and kept them pressed so fine you'd think to look at us Louie and me were working on a dude ranch.

She liked to do embroidery, too. She'd sit by the Wheel for hours and work on a tablecloth or a fancy cushion cover, never looking up unless we called her, like a little old lady I knew in Black Spring that used to be a school teacher and got too old to teach any more.

Only every once in a while she'd put down the needle. "I think I will go and play now," she'd say.

And she'd go outside and roll a little hoop I'd bought her in the market or maybe start bouncing the ball for the jacks. Sometimes if the Wheel wasn't crowded, she'd sit in a car with the dolls, and talk to them like they were people, and tell them stories. But even when she played she never stopped being dignified.

Once in a while I let her take in the money and that made her feel important. And she'd study the change the Arabs gave her to see if any of it was counterfeit, and if a Arab tried to give her a bad coin she'd make him feel sorry.

It was the same way when we went shopping. She'd walk along with me and Louie and find some meat or vegetables she wanted, and she'd ask the price and the man would tell her. And she'd look at him like some of them grand ladies in San Antonio when I was driving, and they'd be standing on the street corner waving and you gave the cab to somebody else.

"You are a cheat," she'd say. And she'd go on to the next stand until she found one where the price was right.

We hadn't heard anything about the pig-eyed man for a while. I wasn't much worried about that, because

I knew he had to come this way to get to the Rio de Oro. There wasn't any other place now he could go. But I sure was wishing I'd find Aziza pretty quick. Things were doing fine with the Wheel. But I didn't know how long it would last. And I sure needed money if I was going to keep on looking. Gasoline way out here was costing plenty.

And then one day we were in a oasis and were drawing a big crowd, when I seen a little merry-go-round come up on a truck, kind of like ours. It was run by a little round fellow with a shiny face and a bald spot on his head big enough to play billiards on, that Louie said was a Armenian.

He stopped and watched the people standing by the Wheel.

"It looks like you do a good business, my friend," he told me in English. All them Armenians talk every language in the world, Louie said. "I think I will stop here, too."

And he pulled up the truck just a couple of feet past us and switched on a loud-speaker, and started the merry-go-round turning.

Well, it wasn't a good merry-go-round. It was built just like one I saw in New York when I was at the camp in New Jersey, the kind the Italians take around and let the kids ride for a penny, just a few scratched-up wooden horses and a lion and maybe a zebra. And it didn't hurt us much. Some of the Arab kids went on it, and maybe a few of the old people that were scared to go on the Wheel.

Louie was mad, though. He said he'd heard about the Armenian in Marrakeesh and that he was a terrible crook.

Louie wanted to do something to the merry-go-round. But I told him the Armenian had as much right there as us.

The Armenian kept trying to be friends, and wanted to give me a little rug—he said he used to peddle them in Paris—but I didn't trust him. A couple of days later we got ready to pull out of the oasis, and sure enough the Armenian started to leave too. And when we got on the road he was following right behind.

I stopped the pickup that pulled the Wheel, and the road was so narrow I knew he'd have to stop, too. I wanted to find out what he was up to.

"I am going to travel with you, my friend," he said. "In this country, it is better if travelers go together."

"Suit yourself," I answered kind of sarcastic. "I don't own the pavement."

We got to the next oasis and set up the Wheel, and he put the merry-go-round right next to us again. I guess he figured Louie being a Arab knew the best place. He did this a few days, and then he wasn't satisfied, he started going ahead of us. And this time he did get a lot of the business, because when we came along everybody'd spent their money on the merry-go-round and didn't have any money left for the Wheel.

"Things are getting rough," I said to Louie one night after we counted the money we took in. "We ain't made enough today to pay the gasoline to run ten miles."

The Armenian kept on like this for a week, maybe. And then I decided we'd have to get to the places before he did or we'd be in a bad way. But that wasn't easy, because he had the merry-go-round in a new truck, and we had to go pretty slow now with our old pickup, because it was getting worn out. That country was terrible on automobiles.

I figured we ought to try it, anyway.

The next morning we were getting ready to go when I heard a big racket at the Armenian's place. I walked over to it and there was a big crowd around, and I see some Arab police tearing up the merry-go-round just the way they did the laundry, ripping the floor boards loose, and even pulling off the heads of the wooden horses.

And then I seen one of the Arabs find something under the floor, and they grabbed the Armenian, and took him down the street toward the jail.

Louie talked to some of the people around, and I asked him what the Armenian'd done.

"He won't bother us now, Joe," Louie said. "They caught him with a lot of counterfeit money."

We went on a couple of days and we did all right again. And then one night we started closing and I woke up Zuleima that was sleeping in her chair right by the Wheel —she wouldn't stay in the hotel without us any more— and I got to thinking about the Armenian.

"I feel sorry for him being in jail," I said to Louie. "Even if he was a counterfeiter."

Louie shakes his head. "He wasn't a counterfeiter."

"I saw them take something from under the floor," I said. "I thought you told me it was counterfeit money."

Louie looked kind of like the organ-grinder monkey when he was taking a peanut out of your pocket and thought you weren't looking.

"I put the money there, Joe," he said. "I did it at night and then in the morning I told the Arab police sergeant. It is not right for a man to annoy us like this Armenian."

I was shocked.

"That's a terrible thing," I said. "You've got to do something quick to get him out."

Louie took off the crank of the engine so nobody could start it going.

"You needn't worry, Joe," he said. "He will not stay in the jail. He will be there only three days longer. Just enough to let us get ahead so he will not bother us any more. Then he will be set free. I have arranged this with the Arab sergeant. I gave him a bundle of the counterfeit money."

I took Zuleima's hand and we walked back with her to the hotel. She went to bed, and I looked in to see if she was all right, and threw a cover over her because it was kind of cool. And then me and Louie turned in, too, and I clicked off the light.

Out in the road a big caravan was passing. I could see the camels marching along, loaded with big bundles of hay and coffee and spices, and the drivers walking beside them, poking them with sticks and hollering "Ous! Ous!"

I lay there thinking.

I heard Louie moving in his bed so I knew he was still awake.

"Where'd you get all that counterfeit money?" I asked.

"From the counterfeiter when you were in the jail for fighting the Legionnaire, Joe," he said. "I stole it from him one day when I came to see you. It is always a good thing to have counterfeit money."

We kept going through deserts and rock country and sometimes maybe across a mountain. And all the time Zuleima'd fix our meals and wherever we stayed, she'd go out and buy flowers and things, and try to make the place

135

look nice. And if the men who cleaned up the rooms didn't do it right, she'd tell them how they were lazy, and take the broom away from them and sweep up the place herself.

Even Louie was afraid of her. Sometimes at night when we came back, if she wasn't too tired, Louie and me'd play a game of Parchesi with her. And Louie would start to cheat and she'd get terrible mad. And he'd look awful worried and say he wouldn't do it any more.

I didn't know what I was going to do with her. A couple of times some missionaries I met said they'd take her. And I thought about it and almost let them keep her.

And then when it came to it and I saw her gripping her dolls and looking at me with her eyes like a hound that's been caught in a fence, I knew I couldn't leave her alone with those strange people. It just didn't seem right.

The country kept getting wilder and wilder. I seen a lot of queer people looked awful mean, and a couple of times things happened like with them Aisawas that made me pretty scared and made Louie keep saying we oughtn't go any farther. It'd been a long time now since we heard anything about the pig-eyed man. But we were almost to the Rio de Oro where I knew he'd taken Aziza, and after coming all this way I sure wasn't going to stop now.

I began watching for her close again. And then we come to the border, right across from the village in the Rio de Oro where we'd heard the pig-eyed man lived.

They had a big French oasis there, and we stopped the Wheel in the square, and were going over to the customs shed to find out about taking it across the line into the Spanish country, when I see a Arab girl, all dressed in silk and a veil, walking with a black man behind her carrying some bundles, like a lot of other Arab women that were doing their shopping.

The girl and the black servant got into a kind of jitney-bus that went over to the Spanish side, and the bus was just starting, when all of a sudden it comes over me.

"It's Aziza!" I called to Louie. "We've found her!"

I run after the bus, but course it's gone. So we get a Arab to take care of Zuleima and the Wheel, and climb in the jeep and drive across the border.

It takes us a while to get through the Spanish police, and then we drive on to the village. It's a little place, just a few houses, but the people all spoke Spanish, and that made it easy for me, account of my having lived with the Mexicans so long.

We asked about the trader's store, and they told us it was about a mile from town, and we drove on out.

It was a big place, all surrounded by a stone wall like a fortress to keep out robbers. And when you went inside the gate there was a garden with a lot of date palms and a big store and a couple of stone sheds like stables for keeping camels and donkeys.

You could see the fellow that owned it was rich.

I looked around for Aziza, but I didn't see any sign of her, and we walked over to the store.

My muscles were getting all kind of tight, I'd been looking for her and the pig-eyed man so long. Now I was there and going to see him, I didn't know what I was going to say. But I sure knew he was going to be surprised to see me way down there in the Rio de Oro.

We went in the store and a black clerk was working

137

there and Louie told him we wanted to see the owner. The clerk pointed off to a house under some palms at the end of the garden.

We walked down the path and stopped in front.

"You better wait here while I talk to him, Joe," Louie said. "If you go in there first I don't know what will happen."

He went through the door and came out again in a minute. He was looking all shaky.

"The pig-eyed man isn't here any more," he said. "He tried to do too many things and lost all his money. He left with all his wives. Nobody knows where he's gone."

Well, it was the same as when the pig-eyed man married Aziza. Like one time I was helping build a ranch house on a place where I was working and the roof fell in and a big beam hit me on the head and they thought I had what they call a concussion.

But when I got to thinking, I couldn't believe what Louie said. I was sure the girl I'd seen in the bus was Aziza. We drove back to the village to look for her and we'd just gone a little way when I saw her with the black servant coming out the door of a Arab house. But when I looked close it wasn't Aziza at all. It was the Arab veil that fooled me. Maybe it had fooled me in Marrakeesh the same way.

I guess if a woman wore those veils inside the house a Arab man'd be lucky to know his own wife.

We drove back across the border to Zuleima and the Wheel. I was all kind of paralyzed again, worse than when the pig-eyed man took Aziza away. Then I had someplace to look, down here in the Rio de Oro. Now he could have taken her anywhere in Africa. All these months I'd spent traveling were for nothing. I'd just have to give up any idea of finding her any more.

And when I thought of her having to stay with that awful man till she died and how there wasn't no hope of doing anything, I felt like a fellow I seen in a court once in San Antonio when a trial was over, and he stood there waiting to hear what the judge was going to say, and the judge told him he was going to be hung.

The only thing left now was to turn around and go back. There wasn't anything south of here but sand. So we got the cars ready again and headed north for Marrakeesh and Bab-El-Kebir.

I sat driving the pickup hardly caring whether we got across the desert or not. Besides Aziza, there were plenty of other things to make me feel bad. Being so far off, I hadn't got any letters from Ma for a long time, and I didn't know how she was with the asthma.

The pickup was wearing out, too, and I was afraid it couldn't make the trip back. And I was getting awful short on money again. There hadn't been many towns down around the Rio de Oro country, and like I said gas way out here cost like it was melted diamonds. I didn't know whether we could make enough to pay our way home or not.

That night when we stopped at a little oasis we heard about a big sheik off in some mountains near us that was having a party for one of his sons that was what they call coming of age—that's a mighty big thing with the Arabs —and Louie said it'd be a good place for us to make some of the money we needed. So we decided to go.

We took the road to the mountains that were all different colors like Arizona, and the grades were so steep and the pickup was behaving so bad that we hadn't gone more than five miles before I was sorry we ever started. The brakes wouldn't hold at all, and every minute I was scared we were burning out the bearings.

We came to a long twisting grade, and I couldn't do anything to make the pickup stop. It was like once when I was riding in a big trailer truck with some cattle down a mountain in the Big Bend country and all the gears went out. We sailed down that mountain in Africa with the Wheel swinging behind us ninety miles an hour. We went past big rocks, all different colors like I said, red and green and purple and yellow, so fast they looked like they all run together. And I just kept hugging that steering wheel, and clamping on the brakes, trying to keep us from rolling over to China.

Zuleima was sitting beside me, and she didn't wink an eye, just sat there like a little statue, as quiet as if she was doing her embroidery.

We made it all right, I don't know how, and got over to the party where the sheik lived down in a kind of canyon all surrounded by red rocks. It was a big affair, like they said, what they call a Mechoui, with a dozen roast lambs sizzling over a fire. There were Arab chiefs from all around, Blue Arabs most of them, with veils and big knives in their belts. But they were smiling now. They were nice fellows when you got to know them. They didn't use the knives at all, except to cut the meat.

It reminded me of the time the rodeo was in Oklahoma City, and the Old Trail Drivers were meeting there and we give them a Texas barbecue.

The sheik was a tall fellow, with a green robe and a

green turban, laughing all the time. And his wives were there, smiling and chattering. He was a special kind of Arab, Louie said, that wasn't so strict about their women not being around. He was awful nice the way he treated everybody. And the people that worked for him, he treated them the same way.

It was like the way Mr. Cullum did that I was working for near Victoria. He was the one that wrote out his name for me on the picture.

The people there ate till they were busting, pretty near, and then the sheik and his wives came over and they rode the Wheel and all the others rode it, too. The Arabs stayed up all night having a fine time and we left in the morning.

There was another steep grade on a mountain right out from the canyon where the sheik lived, worse than the grade we had when we started, only this one was going up. We got along it a little way, pulling the Wheel, when the pickup began rattling and smoking, and pretty soon the whole engine was on fire.

I stopped and jerked open the hood and Louie came up and we tried to put the fire out. But it just got worse. And then I saw it was a goner.

It wouldn't have made any difference even if there hadn't been a fire. The motor was finished and the bearings wouldn't have lasted another day.

So we got our things out fast, and tied the Wheel to some big rocks, and then let the pickup roll down the side of the mountain and burn up.

What we were going to do with the Wheel out there in the middle of the Sahara with nothing to pull it, I didn't know. And then the sheik down in the valley saw

141

what was happening, and he came up riding a horse with a lot of other Arabs, and he said he'd buy it from me as a present for his wives.

Course, he didn't give me hardly anything for it, just a few dollars. But course, he couldn't operate it with gas because there wasn't any, 'way off from everything out there in those mountains. He'd have to make it go by muscle power.

I helped him and the other Arabs roll it down the grade, and we put it in his garden and got ready to go.

Louie and Zuleima climbed into the jeep beside me.

Zuleima looked at the Wheel a long time. "My dolls will be very sad not to ride with me any more," she said.

We started winding up the mountain.

The road swung in a curve and I saw the Wheel down below.

The sheik's wives were sitting in the cars, giggling like little girls, and a couple of big Arab servants were turning it with their hands.

CHAPTER THIRTEEN

We WENT ON FAST NOW without the Wheel. And in a couple of days we came to the little place where we had the big meal with Zuleima's cousins.

Louie found out the cousins were home, and we went to see them and heard her family was back, too, living in a oasis about twenty miles away, so course we decided to take her over.

She was sitting by one of her dolls, sewing a button on one of my shirts, when I had to tell her she couldn't come with us any more.

Her eyes got like the hound in the fence again. But she didn't cry.

143

"I do not wish to go," she said. "I wish to stay with you as your wife always."

I went to the little store where I'd gone before, and bought her the prettiest silk cloth they had so her mother could make her some new robes, and a couple of new dolls, and another game of Parchesi. The old one was getting kind of worn out.

She looked at the old Parchesi board and turned to me with her little face all solemn.

"When you play with Louie, you must be careful," she said. "Louie cheats."

We drove on to the oasis where her family was living now and came to their house. And I gave her a good hug, and then I let Louie take her inside, because I didn't want to get kind of mixed up with the family again and maybe another can of pressed meat.

The last I saw of her she was standing in the door, holding the dolls and waving her hand very dignified, like a little queen.

We got to Marrakeesh not long after and there were a bunch of letters waiting from Ma.

She said she seen in the Houston paper one day they were having a big barbecue for anybody that came from the county Black Spring is in.

And she went and she said she met a lot of wonderful people. And there was a man named Bradley had a shoe store in Houston she liked especial. And this Mr. Bradley had been taking her out a little, and her asthma was a lot better. So she wouldn't be coming over right away.

Well, in no time we were back at Bab-El-Kebir. And we drove down The Street of the Laughing Camel to the little hotel where I stayed the first day I come to the oasis.

The same kids ran after us, yelling their heads off, and the same date sellers were standing in front of their shops. We'd been away almost a year, but hadn't anything changed since we left. There wasn't even a new beggar.

We'd just been at the hotel a hour or so when Louie comes in pretty near busting, he's so excited.

"I just found out, Joe," he says. "Aziza's back in Bab-El-Kebir."

I looked at him like he was crazy.

"It's right, Joe," he says. "She's living with her father and mother in their old house. She's been back almost six months."

He said that right after the pig-eyed man lost his money, he divorced all his wives except his first one, the way rich Arabs do sometimes. The woman lived next door told Louie it was all over town that the pig-eyed fellow would have got rid of Aziza even if he hadn't gone broke, because she was crying all the time. And he hated a crying wife.

Well, for a minute I just stood there, trying to answer something. But I couldn't get no words to come.

That's sure life, ain't it? Here I'd been looking all over North Africa and given up ever finding her, and a lot of the time she'd been right back here where I'd started.

It was like a fellow I knew in the Parts Department that had been working himself up for a year to ask for a ten-dollar raise, and he finally got the nerve and asked the boss. And come to find out, they'd decided a while before to give him a twenty-dollar raise, only of course now they just give him the ten dollars. He was in charge of the motor parts, and you couldn't move a spark plug without his knowing it. That's why they gave him the raise. His

145

name was Kranowitz. That's a Polish name. But everybody called him Mike. He had a cat had six toes on each foot. He brought it to the shop once to show us.

"Where's Aziza now?" I said finally, when I could talk.

"She's over at the Mission, Joe," Louie told me. "She's working today for Miss Peckham."

So course I rushed on over. I saw a billy goat tied outside, and it came up and nuzzled me and I figured it must be Aziza's, it was about the right size the little goat she'd had ought to be. And then I saw Aziza coming around the corner of the house, and start sweeping the sand off the window sills with a brush, Miss Peckham was always so neat.

She was changed a little but was prettier than ever. She was wearing the same kind of gypsy dress with the big belt as when I seen her the last time, and she had a couple more bracelets on her arms and around her ankles.

The goat began maaing and she turned to find out what it wanted. And then she seen me and Louie and she dropped the brush and run and grabbed my hands. It sure made me feel good. And after that she run to Louie and took his hands, too.

She stood there looking at me with the little stars in her eyes and giving them little laughs like the Japanese bells.

"A feather of the hoko bird that lives on the roof of the caid's house fell on my shoulder when I passed this morning," she said. "I knew this meant that today I would have wonderful fortune. For this I will dig up the little worms the hoko wishes until he is so fat he cannot fly any more."

And then her eyes got all milky.

146

The goat maaed louder, and she broke off some grass for it, and then took us inside the Mission.

Miss Peckham was off in town, and we sat there talking. Most of the time she smiled the way she used to, but then she'd get to thinking about the pig-eyed man, and she'd get the far-off look, like the Chinese girl the Ford fellow that spoke at the social meeting brought from Hong Kong.

And she told us all about living with the pig-eyed man and his other wives, how the wives would sit around all day and do nothing except talk and sew fancy rugs, and bathe, and let the black servant women do their hair, and eat French candy and get fat. He was a rich man and they weren't allowed to do any work or even go out of the house except once or twice on Arab holidays when he could take them to a special place in the mosque.

And then she told us how happy she and the other wives were when they heard they were going to be divorced. The pig-eyed man brought them all north on a bus with a lot of Arabs going to Mecca, and took them to the cadi in Bab-El-Kebir, and they got the divorce right there. And then he went off with the first wife to start a new store somewhere in Tunis.

She was still telling us about things when Miss Peckham walked in and she was sure surprised to see us. And then she acted like Louie and me were the son in the Bible that come back, fixing us a chicken and everything you could think of.

Louie asked her about the bums he'd sent her.

Her eyes grew kind of anxious. "I am afraid they may be ill," she said. "They came to the Mission yesterday after I had not seen them for many months and they asked

147

me for money. I gave what I hope was a generous sum, for my check had just come from Fall River, and they gave thanks to our Lord in a beautiful fashion. But today I saw them in the street, and their faces seemed very strange. Though I passed quite close, they did not appear to see me."

She said she had started going to the Ouleds again, and thought she'd got the redheaded woman converted, so she was looking fine.

I took it easy a couple of days, going around the oasis with Aziza and Louie the way we did before, climbing up to the fort with the goat running after her, and going up in the mosque tower with the muezzin and walking out in the desert in the moonlight. It was sure fine to be with her again. It was like old times.

And then I had to decide what I was going to do. I wasn't the kind just to sit around even if I had the money, which I sure didn't. Course I had the machinery for the laundry all stored and waiting for me, and I was thinking maybe I ought to try opening it up again in Bab-El-Kebir, when I got to talking to a couple of Americans at the tourist hotel that were going through on oil business. They'd been traveling all over and they said if they were me they'd go to South Africa or somewhere, anyway in what they call Black Africa. They said the big money now was in Black Africa.

They kept talking about the big town there named Johannesburg that they said was a wonderful place. They said Johannesburg was growing so fast and there was so much money going around, plenty of men that just come there got rich almost before they opened up their suitcases in the hotel.

I talked to some other people and they all told me the same thing. And the more I got to thinking, the more it seemed like the right place to go. So I figured I'd take the laundry machinery I had stored, and start a laundry in Johannesburg.

I figured the laundry ought to go there all right. Just because it didn't do so good in Bab-El-Kebir wasn't any reason it wouldn't be fine somewhere else. If people quit the first time they tried something the world sure wouldn't get very far. Look at the Wright Brothers and the airplane.

I was getting everything collected to start out and I was walking along with Louie to buy some things for the jeep when all of a sudden I felt kind of funny and almost fell down right in the street.

"Looks like I ate something disagreed with me," I said when I was on my feet again. "Like old Gino in Tangiers. I better go on back to the hotel and lay down."

I just about made the hotel and got in bed, and Louie ran out and called the doctor. And by night I didn't know anything that was going on around me, because I was clear out of my head. Seems I got what they call blackwater fever, from some mosquitoes that bit me when we were traveling. I pretty near died, I guess, because that blackwater's one of the worst things in Africa.

I guess I would have died, if Aziza hadn't come and nursed me the way she did. She came every morning as soon as it was light, and stayed till 'way after dark. And sometimes when I was particularly bad, Louie'd make her take his bed, and he'd sleep on a blanket on the floor. Sometimes she stayed two or three days that way.

Louie said I was carrying on pretty crazy a lot of the

time, talking about Black Spring, and the rodeo, and the Parts Department, and some of the rough girls I knowed in the Army, and Ma, and the fellow from the Moose, and reciting some of the poems I wrote.

One time about sunset I'd been having a bad attack, and I woke up feeling awful queer. And I heard voices kind of singing and I smelt perfume like I was in a big flower garden. I didn't know where I was. I thought maybe I'd died and gone to heaven or something.

And then I saw I was in the hotel, and I looked through the window into the courtyard, and there were the six blind holy men that were always around the oasis sitting in front of the door chanting, and the Arab that carried the incense burner was walking up and down waving the incense, and he was chanting, too.

And I saw Aziza by the bed the way she always was and she came over when she saw me move and I asked her what the fellows in the court were doing.

"They are praying for you, *patron*," she said. "I borrowed the money from the moneylender and paid them to pray for three days. Miss Peckham is praying, too. But I do not know whose prayers God likes the best, Miss Peckham's or the holy men. And I thought this way God would be sure to listen."

I guess I was sick bad over a month. And all the time Aziza just stayed there, giving me my medicine and taking care of me every minute.

And when I had the fever she'd fix my pillow and bathe my forehead. And when her hands touched me they'd be so soft and delicate it was like a little breeze shaking the leaves on a tree in summer, so light you could hardly tell anything was there at all.

And I'd lay in my bed and watch her go around on tip-toe, and I'd think about the way I'd looked for her in the skyscraper country, and down in the Sahara with the Blue Arabs, and how I'd do it again because she was sure worth everything I did and more, too.

You know how it is when you're sick and people take care of you, in a couple of days you get to appreciate them more than if you seen them for ten years when you were well. I met a girl once worked in the dime store in San Antonio and she said she was going to get a job as a nurse in a hospital. She said she had a girl friend that quit the dime store for a hospital and in six months she married a man had a chicken ranch worth two million dollars.

I guess I'd have found out how I felt about Aziza before, when she was working in the laundry, except then she was just a kid sixteen and I didn't think of her that way. Like I told the U.S. Consul, I wasn't a cradle snatcher.

But now she'd been married and, I don't know, she wasn't a kid any more. She was grown up and different.

Course, I've went with lots of girls when I was a cow-boy and in the Army, tramps mostly. When you're a cowhand or a cabdriver that's just been to the fifth grade you don't figure on going around with Miss Rockefeller.

The only girl I'd thought of marrying was the one that worked in the diner where the drivers ate, and it turned out she was married to a fellow worked as a bartender in a Greek fish restaurant in Dallas. And Aziza was a hundred times nicer than her.

I didn't have nothing to do all the time I was sick, just working crossword puzzles I got out of Miss Peckham's newspapers, so I wrote some poems. I wrote a poem about

151

driving a cab and the things you see in town that way, and one about the Parts Department, using the names of all the parts in a automobile and making them rhyme. That was a good one.

And I did one about the war, the time I found the wounded fellow that wanted the water. I read that one to Aziza and she burst out crying. I had more time to write poems than I ever did before in my life.

And then one day I watched Aziza getting the drops ready I had to take every few hours and I wrote a poem about her. It was all about how I had a cow in a herd that used to follow me around everywhere. And then the cow got sick and had to take some medicine, and wouldn't take it from nobody but me. And now I was just like the cow, all the time following Aziza around the room with my eyes, and I wouldn't take my medicine from nobody but her.

I don't remember all of it, but it was one of the best poems I wrote. It had some fine verses, about violets and flowers and things. One of my buddies from Algiers that was going through stopped in to see me and he said it was as good as any of them verses they have on a Christmas card. And I seen some fine poems there.

I sat up in bed and read it to Aziza, and the little stars come in her eyes more than I ever seen them before, like one night in Africa I went up in a bomber over the mountains and there were so many stars you couldn't see the sky hardly.

And then when I come to the end where I had a couple of verses all about her, she burst out crying again like when I read her about the fellow that wanted the water. Only this time she was feeling happy instead of sad.

CHAPTER FOURTEEN

W E GOT MARRIED a couple of weeks after, as soon as I
could walk around. We had the wedding over at the Mission, pretty close to sunset when it wasn't so hot.

Miss Peckham gave Aziza a beautiful dress they'd sent
from Fall River a couple of years ago, just in case somebody got married, all white silk with a white veil and white
slippers. The only Arab thing she kept on was a couple of
big silver bracelets full of green stones. She sure looked
beautiful. And the little Bedouin girl that used to work in
the laundry and had come back to Bab-El-Kebir for a
while was the bridesmaid.

Louie was best man, and he was all dressed up in a American suit—I didn't know where he got it—with a stiff collar that pretty near choked him to death. He looked like one of them little monkeys in a zoo when they dress them all up to sit down at a table for a kid's party.

I didn't want to ask Aziza's father and mother to come after what they done to her about the pig-eyed man, but Miss Peckham said they had to be there. The father wanted me to pay him a lot of money, but all I gave him was fifty dollars.

A hour or so before the wedding was going to start, I saw him and the old woman coming on a couple of donkeys all slicked up, leading another donkey all polished up the same way. He grinned at me and kept pointing to the donkeys. I couldn't understand what he was saying, so I called Louie.

"He says they are the three donkeys he bought with the money you gave him, Joe," Louie told me. "He says they are beautiful donkeys. He would like you to take a ride."

Course I wasn't taking any donkey ride just when I was going to my wedding.

Well, in a little while Aziza and me went into the church, and Miss Peckham married us. And then we went in the Mission house. It was dark now and Miss Peckham had the place fixed up awful pretty with candles and lamps. There was a big table in the dining room all set with a couple of big turkeys, and three or four kinds of potatoes, and pies and cakes enough to founder a mule, and Arab dishes like cous-cous, too.

There was fourteen people sat down at the table. There were three of my buddies in Algiers that come down for the wedding. And there was the fat woman that worked in the laundry and the one that looked like a gypsy, and three young Arab girls that were special friends of Aziza's, and one of them brought her little brother. And everybody started to eat, and my buddies and them two old women sure dug in.

Aziza's goat come into the room in the middle and got all excited and knocked over a lamp that was on a stand, but Louie put out the fire before it hurt anything, and it was all right.

And then Aziza did a dance that they said was a wedding dance, at first waving her head back and forth slow and clapping her hands, and then whirling around and stamping her feet like a gypsy. And then she and me sat down on a kind of big red pillow they call a wedding cushion. And then all the neighbor Arab girls that lived in the houses near there came in and marched around the room, playing ladies' drums and singing Arab songs, with that funny Arab music sounds like when you play on a comb.

After that the Army buddy of mine who came to see me when I was sick, a Irish fellow we called Red that used to be in all the company shows, sang *My Wild Irish Rose* and *Mother Machree*. And then he did a singing and ventriloquist act, making voices come from everywhere. And the goat put its head in the door just then and he made it sound like the goat was singing *Take Me Out to the Ball Game*. And everybody pretty near died laughing.

Louie left after the singing was finished, because he said he had to get somewhere early, I didn't know why.

A crowd of Arab people were waiting outside, and we let them come in now, and besides all the things left from the meal we had lots of hamburgers and franks and Orange Drink.

And then I went to the door with Aziza to go over to the hotel where I had a nice room for us. And all the girls started drumming again and Red and my other buddies began singing and everybody throwed rice.

It was sure a fine affair.

I was talking to Louie a couple of days later and I remembered about his leaving so early and I asked him why he did it.

He looked kind of funny. "An American that was in the big hotel lent me the suit I was wearing," he said. "I had to get it to his room by nine o'clock when he came back from a visit to the ruins outside Bab-El-Kebir. If I had not returned it on time he would have been very angry. He did not know he had lent it to me."

We stayed in the hotel about a week, I guess, getting things ready to start for Johannesburg. Being sick hadn't changed my mind at all about going there. And I had talked it over with Aziza and asked her what she wanted to do.

She looked at me the way she did the day I read her the poem. "Wherever you are I wish to be beside you," she said.

It was like them pictures of Ruth and Naomi I seen in the Bible.

They call the town we were going to Joburg but its real name is Johannesburg, for a fellow that was named Johann. That's like Washington, D.C., is named for George Washington.

Well, it was just the same as when I was starting the laundry or going off with the Wheel into the Atlas Mountains. People told me I was crazy making a trip like that all the way across Africa, that we'd get ourselves killed sure. They said the Atlas was bad enough but this country where we were going was ten times worse; if we had a accident, with all the lions and leopards and the bad black people around we'd be done for. They told me there were tribes you had to pass in the jungle that would tear your car apart while you were sleeping to make spears and arrows out of the metal. And that way even if you wasn't killed by the black men, without a car you'd just plain starve to death.

Louie and me had figured on being together whatever I did, but about this he talked the same as the others. His little monkey face was awful worried. "If we go I do not think we will come back, Joe," he said. "This is terrible country. And there is too much happening now with the black people. You stay in Bab-El-Kebir, Joe. I will fix things with my friends for us to go into the black market. And we will not be caught like that stupid Arab who worked for the Egyptian."

Course I argued him out of it. The way I figure, you can only die once.

A few days later we piled the laundry machinery into a trailer hooked onto the jeep, and Aziza gave the goat to a nice old Arab, and we all went off to tell Miss Peckham good-by. Miss Peckham said when we got settled in Joburg she'd come down to visit us, because she'd always wanted to see the other parts of Africa. She had a sister that was a missionary in South Africa, wasn't more than a hundred miles from where we'd be, and a sister in Liberia, too, out near them American rubber plantations.

And then Aziza and me and Louie climbed in the jeep again, and I put my foot on the starter and we're off for Johannesburg.

It was rough going the way we went, even for a jeep. We went straight south and at first it was all right. The roads were good and you could drive along fast. And then all of a sudden the good roads were gone, and all you had to go by were the tracks the cars ahead of you had made in the sand.

Now we were married, Aziza was just like she used to be when she worked in the laundry. She'd sit up by me in the jeep, chattering and singing. And when we'd stop she'd jump out and run off in the desert or the oasis, wherever we were, and she'd always find a flower or a pretty stone. She was learning English now out of a book Miss Peckham gave her, and she sure learned it fast. A lot of the fancy words she could say better than me.

After a while the country began to be different. Now it was big palm hammocks and cactus and thorn trees stretching out for miles and miles. There was water sometimes, too. Maybe you'd be camping near a dry river bed like in Texas, nothing but stones and gravel all around, and then at night there'd be a storm, with terrible thunder and lightning, and in the morning the river bed'd be roaring. And when you had to go across, the water'd come 'way up over the floorboards.

Sometimes even the jeep couldn't get through. You'd go down too deep in a mudhole, and you'd have to wait all day till a truck came along or a native with a couple of big oxen, and they pulled you out.

And then everything changed again and as far as you could look there was nothing but miles and miles of grass, so high you couldn't have seen a man if he was fifteen feet tall. There'd be all kinds of animals grazing in front of you. But you wouldn't see just two or three. It'd be more like a couple of hundred, zebras and giraffes and ostriches and then maybe a single antelope, white as snow. And then something would give them a scare and they'd all run off making a noise like a tornado.

At night you could hear the leopards screaming. And one morning we saw three lions cross in front of us, just like it was a zoo.

We kept heading south. And then we met a couple of American Army trucks that were going through to what they called the Gold Coast, and they said we'd better come with them, even if it was a long way round. They'd heard over the radio there'd been some bad washouts in Nigeria that was ahead of us, and we couldn't get through. We drove with them a couple of days. Like the Armenian said, it was a good thing to travel together in that country.

We began to see jungle now. You'd climb a mountain and come down on the other side and right away you'd begin going through trees a couple of hundred feet high, all tangled up with vines big as your arm, and so dark you'd think you were driving through a tunnel.

And then there'd be some big baboons standing in a wide place waiting to throw a stick against the windshield when you passed.

The people weren't the same now, either. They weren't Arabs any more. They were all black, big tall fellows without much clothes, just a pair of cloth trunks maybe, or a piece of burlap. Their faces and bodies were all cut with little scars, and the women had colored stones under their skins, so it looked just like tattooing. The men were all carrying spears or big throwing knives that could cut your head off three hundred feet away.

Every once in a while you'd hear drums beating, and you didn't know what it meant, whether the black people were just passing the time of day, or whether they were getting ready to kill you.

We came to a river one morning at the edge of a big forest where there was a ferry made of three big canoes. The road branched here and the trucks were going farther down the river. So we left them and got the jeep onto the ferry. Some big black men started pushing with long poles, and pretty soon we came to the other side where there was a village made of straw houses that looked just like beehives.

A couple of black soldiers in uniform were waiting when I drove onto the dock, and they signaled me to stop. And then a Englishman came up, a tall fellow wearing a helmet and shirt and shorts, all so white and shiny it blinded you, pretty near. He was shaved so clean and looked so neat you'd figure he was all dressed up to go to a party, instead of being out there in the middle of the jungle.

He took our passports and I asked him where we are.

He studied my papers and looked me and Louie and Aziza over a long time. He's nice, but I could see he was a kind of nervous fellow, always worrying.

"You are in the village of Kimali," he said. "In the British mandated territory of Togoland under the special administration of His Majesty's Crown Colony of the Gold Coast. This is Equatorial Africa. Do not drink the water unless it is boiled or filtered. And treat the African population with courtesy. If you have trouble send word to the nearest police office at once. I hope it will not be necessary. Good luck."

He stamped our papers with a rubber stamp, and called out to a young English fellow sitting in a little straw shelter near us, writing in a book. "Three arrivals by car at 4:56. Two male, one female. All foreigners."

It was sure funny hearing him call me a foreigner. Course he was the foreigner all the time.

CHAPTER FIFTEEN

We left the Englishman and rode all day through the palm hammocks and thorn trees they call the Orchard Bush Country. And about sunset we came to another river with a ford across it where we could see a big village on the other side.

Some crocodiles were laying along the bank and every once in a while you'd see a log floating down. And then the log opened its mouth and it was a crocodile, too.

We were driving in the middle of the river with the water around us maybe a foot deep, and I was keeping a sharp eye out for any of those logs, when all of a sudden the jeep went down in a hole so hard it felt like I'd broke my neck.

I jumped out in the river to look. The jeep was sure in bad shape. The front wheels were twisted every which way and the bumper was laying on the bottom.

I shook my head. "This ain't our lucky day," I said. "We've broke a axle."

I was trying to think what to do when I saw a big crocodile a little way up the river come swimming down towards us. I helped Aziza climb out of the car in a hurry and took her by the arm. The three of us splashed through the water over to the bank.

Right by the shore there was a kind of trading post like they have around New Mexico in the Indian country, with a few colored fellows standing in front. They went in the store and got some ropes, and we waded into the river again, and dragged the jeep up on the land.

By this time a Arab was outside waiting for us, a big man dressed in a blue-and-white striped burnoose and a red hat, with a puffy face and a stomach that would have got him a job as the fat woman in a circus if he'd have been a lady. He looked just like one of those fat fellows smoking a water pipe you used to see on a pack of Turkish cigarettes.

I didn't like him at first because he was so fat. But when he started talking I saw he was all right. It was like the fat fellow, when I was a kid, that ran the butcher shop in Black Spring. When I went there the first time, I didn't like him at all. And then we got to be good friends and whenever I come to the store he always gave me some extra soup meat for Ma. The Arab's name was Suleiman.

I asked him how long it would take to get a new axle, and he said a couple of months, anyway.

I told him that was terrible, that we had to get on to Joburg, and I asked him if he had a place where we could stay for a night or two while I tried to figure things out.

And he said he had a couple of rooms he could spare, so we went inside.

It was a big store with a lot of porches all covered with thatch, and there's everything inside, picks and shovels for prospecting gold, and the counters they use looking for uranium, and tools for cocoa and banana plantations, and guns for hunting elephants. And besides that it's filled with U.S. Army surplus, blankets and lanterns, and brooms and mess kits, and army boots and dungarees. I guess there ain't a place in the world now where you can't get U.S. Army surplus.

The fat fellow went with us to show us our rooms in a kind of little hotel he'd built, and then invited us over to his own place in back of the store that was all fixed up in fancy Arab style. His stomach was so big that with every step he took you could almost hear it bump.

He smiled at us very friendly and poured out some Arab coffee that was just like molasses.

"You come from New York, Sidi?" he asked me. Sidi is the way they say Mister in Arab.

I shook my head. "I been there," I said. "But I come from Texas."

"I have a cousin who went to Texas," he said. "He lived in a place high in the mountains. I think it was called Denver."

We talked awhile and then he walked over and turned on a radio. It started playing some African music but it wasn't working right, so I took a screwdriver and opened it up and had it fixed in no time.

He thanked me and went into another room where I could hear Arab women talking, and comes out carrying one of them old-time phonographs with a big horn shaped like a morning-glory.

"This belongs to my wives, Sidi," he said. "They like this talking machine very much. But it has been broken for a long time. Maybe you can fix this, too."

Well, wasn't nothing much wrong, and I fixed it easy, and he took it back to the women. And they started it playing some funny Arab song, and I could hear them all giggling. And then the fat Arab invited Aziza to go back with them, and I could hear her talking to the wives, and laughing and giggling, too.

And then Aziza and Louie and me went off to a little dining room, and a black boy brought us supper.

We were still eating when the fat Arab came in and sat down by me.

"I have been thinking, Sidi," he said. "This country is growing fast, and I am starting a new store at Yembasi. That is a hundred miles from here, up the river. I need someone like you who speaks English and is good with the machinery. How would you like to go up the river and manage this store?"

Well, I knew I'd be months waiting for the axle. And like I said, I make up my mind quick. So I told him I'd forget Johannesburg for a while anyway and take the job.

Next day I was down at the ferry talking to a fellow going through with some big trucks loaded with cocoa. He was one of them little English fellows they call a Cockney, had a red face kind of like a hamburger before it's cooked. I told him where I was going, and he shook his head.

"You wouldn't catch me up there for a thousand pounds, you wouldn't," he said. "There's too many bloomin' wild places in this 'ere part of Africa. And they tell me this 'ere Yembasi country's the worst."

Another little Cockney with him nodded. "'E's got it right. It's a terrible country. Full of leopard-men that goes around at night wearing leopard skins and claws. And then in the morning the police finds you dead under a palm tree, all clawed up. The way I 'ears in a pub down at Accra, ain't two months ago they killed the foreman of one of them big manganese mines they just opened there. And the police buried him right on the spot, instead of sending him back to England the way they allus does, because they didn't want his wife to see the body."

Course, I didn't pay no attention to a couple of funny Cockneys, and in a few days we're all ready to start out. We went down to the wharf where a canoe that looked big as a destroyer, pretty near, was waiting for us, all loaded up with Army surplus.

There were eight big black men holding paddles, and a black fellow named Gwani, one of those kind of giants you seen in the movies, pretty near seven feet tall, a kind of mournful-looking fellow wearing a khaki coat with brass buttons and khaki pants like a uniform. I guess he'd been a soldier once.

He had three scars like new moons on each of his cheeks and the other black fellows said the scars meant he had king's blood in him.

There was a Indian worked in a machine shop in San Antonio that had a couple of scars and he'd have been a king if he'd stayed with his people. But he said he got his scars when what they call a Hungarian come at him with a chisel.

I climbed in the canoe and pretty soon this Gwani said

something and the eight black men got ready. And then somebody began singing a African song and the black men dipped their paddles all together, and we started up the river.

We traveled all day without stopping. It was pretty, going along the water, with the black men chanting and keeping time with their paddles. The river went through country like we'd been coming through, sometimes grass so high it scared you, and sometimes the jungle, so thick it was like a green stone wall.

There were big crocodiles everywhere on the bank now. When they opened their mouths, full of horrible teeth, they made me think of the caves I seen out in New Mexico with the white stone things growing from the ceiling and the floor. Families of hippos were playing and splashing in the water, just like a bunch of dogs. And once a herd of elephants came out of the trees, to get a drink of water, I guess. And they saw us and moved away.

Every once in a while we'd hear tom-toms going, and in a minute we'd pass a little straw village where you could see black women wearing nothing but a couple of banana leaves cooking over a fire or pounding meal. And then we'd pass some big canoes like ours or a launch going up to the mines.

We stopped at sunset and camped in what they call a rest house, because a road crossed there and the government builds the rest places for the travelers so they can sleep out of the rain.

It wasn't really a house, just a kind of straw lean-to, and when we came we found some other people there already, a couple of Englishmen from a big manganese mine close by and a British Army captain and a man looking for

uranium, and one of those science fellows studying but-
terflies.

We all made friends and put our food together.

At first Aziza was awful shy. She wasn't used to being
with so many English people. But she was the only
woman, and the Army captain, a big English fellow looked
like he had a broomstick in his back but was real polite,
come and asked her if she'd do the cooking.

She smiled at him kind of embarrassed. "I have cooked
only for the Arabian people and for Yance," she said. "My
cooking it is very bad. But if you wish I will try."

She went to a big iron pot standing over a fire in the
middle of the room, and pretty soon she had all the things
thrown in, and made a kind of stew. And I took a spoon-
ful and it was wonderful. And then she passed it around
in tin dishes we had, giving everybody a smile, and looking pretty as a picture. It reminded me of the way the girl
did at the diner in San Antonio when all the cabdrivers
came in at once.

And then all the people in the rest house asked for seconds, and after that the English captain stood up and they
gave Aziza three cheers.

We started out before daybreak and went on most of
the day, and then I heard the tom-toms going again and
we came in sight of Yembasi, a lot of beehives like the
others, only these hives were square instead of round.

We tied up at the bank and started going over to the
trading post they'd just finished. A lot of natives were
gathered in a open place in front of the houses, and I
knew something was going on. And then I saw a bunch of
the black men pulling at some ropes like what they call a

168

tug of war, only this time the ropes were fastened around the neck of a black girl.

It made me feel pretty awful because it looked like they were choking her to death, and I asked Gwani if we couldn't do something.

He shook his head. "They are not choking her, Master. They are giving her a divorce. Walk closer and you will see, Master."

I came up to her and saw that she had on a big brass collar, with the ropes tied to it in a couple of places. They weren't pulling at her neck at all. They were really trying to pull the collar open.

The black fellows kept working till the collar finally spread enough so they could take it off. And then the girl looked kind of worried, and walked down a path toward one of the beehive houses.

"She is divorced now," said Gwani. "Here in Yembasi sometimes when a girl is married her husband puts on her one of these great collars so heavy that she cannot run away. So when he no longer wishes her as a wife, he and the others come with the ropes and pull it apart. The collar is so strong it is the only way."

It was kind of the same as when I was in a jewelry store in Dallas once getting a clock fixed and a big blond-haired woman come in. She told the clerk she was getting a divorce and wanted to get rid of her wedding ring, but her finger had got fat around it and she couldn't get it loose. So they had to cut it off with a file and a big hacksaw. They was kind of rough people in the store and they handled that woman like they were shoeing a horse.

We walked on and I got a chance to see the natives

close now. Some of them were pretty near naked and had colored feathers in their ears that made them look like wild men, but a lot of them had been working up in the manganese mines, and some of these fellows were wearing old pants and shirts.

The women were mostly wearing nothing but the banana leaves, but a few had what looked kind of like the Japanese dresses they call kimonos.

We came to the trading post a few minutes after that and the black men carried over everything from the canoe. It was right on the water where a narrow river came down into the big one, a store about like Suleiman's only smaller, with a thatched roof and rooms at the back for us to stay.

We'd been there a little while when the chief of the village came over, a little old man with silver-white hair and all shriveled up like a cowhide that's laid out a long time in the sun. He had a big green stone in his nose and a leopard skin over his shoulders. He was a nice old man and gave us half a dozen bantam chickens to show us we're welcome.

His son was with him, a tall, skinny young fellow maybe about twenty, had a purple cloth tied around his head like a Arab turban. His chest was bare, but it had the colored stones under the skin like I seen before so that it looked like fancy tattooing. You could tell right away he wasn't nice like the old man. He had a hollow face, kind of mean and tricky, with shifty eyes that had too much of the whites showing. He'd never look at you straight.

He reminded me of a fellow that was in the rodeo once was always stealing shirts and things from the lockers. There was a long string of keys hanging down from his neck. But I found out he didn't have a single lock for them to open. His name, they said, was Omambe. The name of the fellow that stole the shirts was Tex.

I gave them both some cans of tomatoes and corned beef, and they went off happy.

But Louie looked worried. "I do not like the chief's son, Joe," he said. "I think he will make trouble."

We got a bad scare that very first night. We were eating supper when all of a sudden I heard a terrible beating of drums outside. And I looked through the window and there were about thirty wild black fellows with their faces painted in white and blue circles. They were all carrying clubs and bows and arrows and they shook them at the house like they were crazy.

I went for my gun but Gwani told me it was nothing.

"Someone has died in the village, Master," he said. "They are driving away the evil spirits of the dead."

We opened up the store next day and put out the Army surplus things and we did all right. Some of the black men had plenty of money from working in the mines, or cutting the big mahogany trees and sending them down the river. We sold a lot of canned goods and lanterns and sheets.

And we had a lot of parachutes and Coast Guard signal flags, and the black women made things to wear out of them. It was funny to see them going around with nothing on except little pants that said with the signals "Follow me," or "I'm on fire," and some just had printed, "Property of U.S. Government."

We had a lot of cans of insecticide and the pumps to spray it with. We were selling them fine because there were so many bugs around, and then one day a Hausa trader came along with a kind of barge full of them he'd bought from the surplus, too. And he was selling them 'way below what we were charging, and course we couldn't sell any more.

I was awful worried because I knew Suleiman had plenty more at his place, and it looked like we were going to be stuck with the whole lot.

And then one morning I noticed some of the black people were coming to buy our pumps again, and the Hausa trader was gone.

"I'm sure glad that fellow's not around any more," I said to Louie. "I wonder what happened to him."

Louie made a pile of the cans so the black people could see them first thing when they came in the store.

"The Hausa left in a hurry," Louie said. "He was in front of the chief's house yesterday, showing the chief how the pumps worked. When his back was turned I emptied out the insecticide he was using and put in gasoline instead. And when he started pumping on some ant-hills by the doorway, I lit a cigarette and threw away the match. The fire burned a big hole in the front of the house. They would have killed the Hausa, but I told them the English police would come and be very angry. So they let him go away. The chief thanked me many times. If I hadn't helped them put out the fire, his house would have burned to the ground."

After that we sold every can we had, and when we couldn't get any more everybody kept on using the empty pumps just the same. The black people said they killed the bugs fine.

Things went along pretty quiet for a while. I kept thinking up new ideas to boost business for the store. I started some contests, like guessing the beans in the jar when I had the laundry, only counting ants instead. And once I had a fight between a scorpion and a big spider I kept in a box with a screen over it like I seen once in a clothing store in Texas. The fight lasted pretty near two weeks and brought a lot of people to watch. The spider won.

At night I'd help Aziza with the English book. Like I said, she was doing wonderful. She was wearing American clothes all the time now. Only once in a while she'd put on one of her Arab dresses and take out her Arab drum and play and sing the way she used to in Bab-El-Kebir. But she was always surprising me.

One night I was inside the house when I saw her running in all excited.

"Come quick, Yance!" she called. "The fairies are dancing!"

I ran out with her and looked where she pointed.

It was the lightning bugs, all different colors the way they are in Africa, flickering like somebody was throwing chips of colored glass.

It was too dry for lightning bugs in the desert and she'd never seen one before in her life.

Another night I'd had to go down the river in a canoe a little way and I got back and saw her drinking some kind of blue-colored water out of a glass.

She sort of jumped when I come in, and then smiled kind of embarrassed when I asked her what she was drinking.

"It is a prayer given me by one of the holy men in Bab-El-Kebir," she said. "He wrote out the prayer on a piece of paper and gave it to me to use if I was afraid you would divorce me. Today I saw the girl again that had the brass

173

collar taken from her neck, and tonight when I was alone I grew worried. So I took the paper and put it in a glass of water and drank the ink as the holy man told me. And that way I would be protected by the prayer."

The nights were sure wonderful there with Aziza, but with those big trees and the jungle so near it made you feel kind of queer, like something was always getting ready to happen.

You could always hear things crawling in the roof thatch, and once in a while you'd hear a terrible wrestling around up there, maybe a lizard fighting a snake.

Out in the river a crocodile would splash, or up on the bank a leopard 'd scream. And sometimes 'way off you'd hear the roar of a lion. And in the village the drums 'd be beating so loud and you'd hear voices hollering so wild you'd think all the black people in Africa were going crazy.

And Aziza and me'd talk about Bab-El-Kebir and Miss Peckham, and Black Spring, and how I hoped it wouldn't be too long before she'd meet Ma.

And then we'd put the mosquito nets around the bed, and go to sleep.

CHAPTER SIXTEEN

THERE WERE A LOT OF WHITE PEOPLE coming through on
their way to the mines, engineers and mechanics and fellows like that, and a few white men going up to the villages.

A launch ran up the river three times a week, and then
we heard they'd even started a airplane service from Accra.
That's the big town of the Gold Coast where the English
governor stayed that ran Yembasi and all this Togoland
country.

There were plenty of Arabs and Hindus, too, traders

that had groceries and stores, and there were half a dozen of them lived with their families right at the edge of Yembasi.

One day the launch came up bringing a bunch of Arabs, and next morning Louie turned up with a pretty Arab girl had a fancy robe on and was giggling all the time behind her veil.

"This is my sister, Joe," he said.

She didn't look any more like him than the two that worked in the laundry in Bab-El-Kebir. She stayed in the house a couple of weeks and then one morning she was gone. He sure had a lot of sisters.

All the white people that traveled on the launch and stopped for the night stayed with me and Aziza. We had a separate little building with three or four rooms for them near one end of the store. And one day a fellow came, so quiet and kind of English I didn't know for a couple of hours that he was a American.

He was a middle-aged man, and he was working for a American company, selling engineering supplies. I hadn't seen a American since I'd been in Yembasi, and I stayed up so late talking to him Aziza came to find out if I was all right.

You only had to be with this fellow a minute to see he did plenty of thinking.

Well, the tom-toms started going in the village like they did every night, and we began talking about the black people's funny ways.

The engineer said he'd been in Africa fifteen years, working for different companies, and he'd had time to see a lot. And he'd been figuring more and more it wasn't right just to sell the black people things and use them to make a profit. He said if we made money from them it was our duty to civilize them and give them the same advantages we had in America.

"These poor devils are still up in the trees," he said. "It's our job to help them down."

Course it was the same as what the Consul told us that time about showing them how Americans did things, and just the way I'd been thinking ever since I come to Yembasi.

The engineer said the way they were doing down in Liberia where there were a lot of Americans was to start little clubhouses, kind of like a Y.M.C.A., and have moving pictures and what they call community sings, and lots of athletics and field meets.

I told him about Miss Peckham and the Mission, and how she said maybe she'd come down for a visit. And he said he wasn't crazy about missionaries, but if they didn't get cracked on religion some of them done a lot of good. And he'd seen for himself they sure knew how to start those clubhouses.

After he left in the morning, what he told me about being up in the trees and what the Consul said kept sticking in my mind, and the more I thought the more I figured maybe I ought to do something.

And I talked it over with Suleiman when he came up on the launch and he said it was a good idea. He said the Koran taught you to be charitable and help people. And besides that, the more American things the black people knew about, the more of the Army surplus they'd want to buy.

Louie was writing Miss Peckham to thank her for some presents—she kept sending him things all the time—so I thought I'd write her, too, about what the eng ...er said. Even if she didn't have many converts, she sure d a nice mission building, and maybe she'd have some is.

I'd hardly put the letter on the launch whe .ere was a letter from her right back, all excited, telling what I ought to do. She wrote me every few days and sent me a lot of books and papers, how to get a clubhouse going and that kind of thing. And she said she was so interested she was trying to arrange to get down to visit her sister in Liberia and stop off in Yembasi a few days on the way.

And first thing I knew the launch brings a telegram saying she's taking the plane to Accra and'll be arriving in a week.

I'd got awful fond of Miss Peckham in Bab-El-Kebir, even if I wasn't a church-going fellow. And I'd sure be glad to see her again. And I knew Aziza'd be the same way. In Africa that's about the hardest thing there is, not seeing anybody you know. It's like when you're out West riding fences all by yourself for a week, maybe, you get so lonesome if somebody you know comes along you'll kiss him, pretty near, even if he's somebody you'd have shot at in a town.

It ain't long before we hear the launch that Miss Peckham is on coming up the river, and Aziza and me and Louie go down to the dock. We see her by the rail, wearing her black dress and black hat and carrying a little black parasol. But she's got a flower pinned on the dress and she looks real pretty.

She smiled when she saw us, and put up the parasol and walked with us to the store. I never seen her so happy, though she was a little shaky.

"It was my first airplane," she said. "I am still trembling from the ride. Though it was wonderful to be up in the sky so near to our Lord."

She looked down at her flower kind of apologetic. "I hope the Lord will pardon my wearing this flower. The stewardess of the airplane pinned it to my dress before I could prevent her. It was so beautiful I did not have the heart to take it off."

She stopped on the path to look out over the river with the jungle on the other side and the crocodiles laying in the sun.

"It was wonderful on the boat to see God's handiwork," she said. "The great trees and the crocodiles and the monkeys and all His other creatures. Once when we were at the shore I saw a great leopard hiding in a tree, and its eyes were like the fiery eyes of Satan the day the Lord cast him out from Heaven. But I did not tell the crew. I was afraid they would kill him, and after all he, too, even though misguided, is a creature of the Lord."

We came to the store and showed her where she was going to stay.

She opened up one of her suitcases and took out some packages. "This first one is a present for my son, Mohammed," she said, giving it to Louie. "It is a pair of gold shirt studs sent by my friends in Fall River. They know Mohammed well. He is as dear to my friends in Fall River as he is to me. This is a dress for Aziza. And this book is for Mr. Cullum here. It is a book of the Holy Land. It shows with many beautiful pictures everywhere that our Lord wandered."

I showed her around the village, and every beehive house we passed where the black people were working outside her face would get all bright. I told her what the engineer had said about the black people and what I'd been thinking, too. She kind of wanted to start a mission, but I didn't know whether Suleiman would like it, he being a Mohammedan. But I knew he wouldn't have no objection if it was just a kind of clubhouse. So in the morning we picked out a nice open spot on the river and began putting up a place right away.

We got it built in a few days. It wasn't anything but a log frame, covered over with thatch to make the roof and walls. Looked kind of like a tobacco barn back home that they'd covered all over with hay. And inside we put around some rough kind of benches like in a church for people to sit on and a kind of platform for anybody that was making a speech.

Miss Peckham looked at it kind of like a mother cat that has her first kitten.

"I think it would make the Lord very happy to open it with a community sing," she said. "I rode on the airplane to Accra with a Reverend Mr. Pell who is the chief of a mission in Accra, though, alas, not of our denomination. He said the community sing was the key to the hearts of these simple black children, they love music so. And God gave them the voices of his angels."

Course I said all right and in no time she had Louie and Gwani going around collecting the black men and bringing them over to the clubhouse to start practicing the songs.

They didn't ask the women, just the men. Because the men were awful strict about keeping the women off to themselves, and none of the women were allowed to come.

The black men hurried over, a lot of them with the colored feathers in their ears and nothing much on except a strip of cloth around their waists. With the queer tattoo-ing on their bodies and faces they looked fierce enough to scare off a lion. They sat down kind of uneasy, wondering what was going to happen.

Miss Peckham had brought one of those little organs like the country people used to have out in Texas, and we'd put it up on the platform. She went over to it and then found a songbook. And she stood there looking awful nice, just like the music teacher in Black Spring, the way I seen her once when she was getting ready to give what they call a music recital. You could hear her dress crackling every time she moved.

"The first song we will sing will be *Way Down Upon the Suwanee River*," she said. "I have some lovely slides of the Suwanee River at Bab-El-Kebir that I wish I might have shown to you. Is there anyone in my audience who perhaps can play the mandolin or the banjo? I heard a Glee Club once, when I went to Boston, sing and play *Suwanee River* and it was very beautiful. Perhaps if there are a number who play these instruments we can have not only a Glee Club but a mandolin and banjo club here."

The black people just looked at her awful puzzled. She talked to them some more about the songs they were go-ing to sing, and then sat down at the organ, and began to play *Suwanee River*. And then she sang it, too, in her shaky little voice. Course it wasn't hard to get the black people to sing with her. There ain't nobody in the world can sing like black people. And in a minute they were all smiling and patting their feet, and going fine. And then she played *Kentucky Home* and *Old Black Joe* and after that *Pack Up Your Troubles* and *I'm Always Chasing Rainbows* and all kinds of songs that way.

181

She stopped after a while and turned to me. "I know Mr. Suleiman is, alas, a Mohammedan," she said. "But do you think he would mind if they sang *Onward Christian Soldiers*? I taught it to the Ouleds in Bab-El-Kebir after you went away and they sang it so sweetly. It was like the birds at daybreak."

I couldn't see any objection, so she started it on the organ.

Well, if those black fellows sang before, it was nothing to the way they did *Christian Soldiers*. They pretty near shook down all the thatch. Course, it's a wonderful song. After that they wouldn't sing anything else hardly.

It kind of made me think of what they call a quartet used to sit around the barbershop in Black Spring and they'd never sing nothing but *Sweet Adeline*.

In a couple of days everything in the club was ready and Miss Peckham and Aziza fixed it up with African flowers that had pink and yellow blossoms big as saucers and smelled so sweet they put you to sleep almost. And when it got dark we started things off.

The room sure looked pretty all lit up with oil lamps and lanterns we took from the surplus at the store. Miss Peckham sat up on the platform and Aziza was next to her, wearing the new dress Miss Peckham had brought, all pink what they call chiffon so she kind of looked like one of the flowers on the wall.

Louie and me opened the doors and the black men started coming in, and some of them were sure dressed up.

The chief came first with his leopard skin and the green stone in his nose. And to show who he was a man walked in back of him carrying a fancy stool, and another was carrying a African rug. The man with the rug laid it on the platform, and then the other fellow put the stool on the rug. I figured he was fixing the stool there for the chief to sit on. But that wasn't right. The chief sat down on the rug by it, all solemn and dignified, and nobody sat in the stool at all. It's the way they do in that country.

Right in back of him came his son, Omambe, and he was wearing a leopard skin now, too, and a little skirt all covered with gold embroidery, and course the chain with the couple of hundred keys. You could see he thinks he's pretty fine-looking. He took a place on the rug by his father and he sits there awful smart-aleck, kind of studying everybody that come in with his shifty eyes.

Some of the other men were pretty near naked like when they came to practice the songs, except this time they had strings of beads and shells across their chests and rings of monkey fur around their hands and feet. And their bodies were all polished up with some kind of oil so they shone like a looking glass. A few of them were wearing clothes that were kind of mixed up, a bunch of foxtails hanging around them for pants and maybe a steel helmet and a pair of canvas puttees they bought in the store.

When they got quiet I came to the front of the platform and made a little speech. I tell them what we're trying to do and how it's to make things nicer for them, that it's like the club we had in the Parts Department, kind of where they can enjoy themselves and learn something, too. I had a sign there I'd painted with fancy letters, Yembasi Club. I figured that'd be nice. And I took a hammer and drove in a nail and hung the sign on the wall in back of the platform. And that way it meant that the Club was open, like I seen mayors do at a new racetrack or something. And the chief gets up and says thanks.

And then Miss Peckham made a speech, too, and started the singing.

Well, the black people sang and sang, and every chance that came they switched over to *Onward Christian Soldiers*. It got awful late and finally we went off to bed. But they were still going like they'd just begun.

They liked the singing so much they did it every night. They'd keep it up sometimes till daybreak. And they'd bring their drums, too, and hit pieces of iron together so it'd ring like those things they call triangles a trap drummer back home hits with a stick.

One night we had a terrible storm, so bad Aziza and me and Louie sat up with Miss Peckham because we didn't want her to be worried. The rain came down in sheets, and some trees were falling out in the woods near us, the wind was blowing so hard. And right in the middle of it we could hear the black people singing *Christian Soldiers*.

Miss Peckham listened and her face was all bright.

"It is thrilling to hear these trusting children singing in this terrible storm," she said. "This beautiful song of the Lord gives them strength and so they are not afraid."

I woke up in the middle of the night and the black people were still singing it, more and more excited. They sure liked that song.

I guess it was almost three or four days later when a dried-up old woman that looked like one of the funny-shaped voodoo statues the black people had there came in the store and told Gwani she wanted to see me.

I walked over and I thought she was going to faint, she

was shaking so. She started crying something terrible and then she talked so fast Gwani had to make her go slower so he could understand.

I asked him what was the matter.

Gwani was so tall in his khaki uniform the old woman by him looked like a baby.

"She asks you to stop the singing of the Song of the Marching Soldiers, Master," he told me. "Her son is very sick. She says she wishes her son not to leave her and go into the Land of the Sky."

I looked at the old woman. "Tell her I'm awful sorry about her son," I said. "Tell her I'll ask them to sing quiet after this so they won't bother him any more."

But the old woman shook her head and cried and talked all excited again.

The scars like new moons in Gwani's face kind of flickered. "She says this would do no good, Master. She says only if they stop the Song of the Marching Soldiers will her son not go away to the Land of the Sky. For all the magic of the white people is in this song. And it is terrible magic. She says her son has enemies. And with this magic song they are praying him to death."

Course that was a terrible thing. I'd heard about praying people to death plenty before I started from Bab-El-Kebir. They did it all over Africa. I told Gwani to tell the black people they couldn't sing *Christian Soldiers* any more. And they stopped and the fellow got well right away.

Miss Peckham was kind of disappointed, and wondered what made them quit singing it all of a sudden. But I never told her why.

Sometimes it ain't any use telling people the truth. It

was like a wild duck we had in a little cattle pond in Texas, that'd got blowed out there from the Gulf in a storm and broke his wing and couldn't fly back. Course there weren't any other ducks around and he got awful lonesome and sad. And then one day a fellow happened to come through with one of them painted ducks hunters use, and he gave it to this duck. And the duck'd sit by it all day and quack to it, and was happy as could be. It'd have broke that duck's heart if you'd have told him that his friend was made of wood.

A few days after that about the *Christian Soldiers* the chief's son came into the store. Gwani told me it was him that'd been praying the sick man to death because he wanted the fellow's wife.

He bought a couple of lanterns and some rope and shovels and said he'd pay me next day. But next day came and next week and he never paid at all.

I was going to ask him for the money because course it wasn't mine, it was Suleiman's. But Gwani told me it'd be awful bad if I did. So I didn't say anything. But every time I thought about it I sure got mad.

And then he came in two more times and did the same thing. I kept quiet again, but when the first of the month came around I figured I'd send him a bill the way people do in the States. So I wrote one out and put on it "Overdue" like I seen the furniture stores and places back home write when people ain't paid up, and gave it to Gwani to take to the chief's son's house. Course I knew he couldn't read it, but I told Gwani what it said. Gwani come back in a little while with his face kind of gray, but he had the money.

Whenever the chief's son come after that you can bet

he paid cash. And he didn't laugh and joke with me like the others. He'd just hand me the money and give me a look with his mean eyes so hot and red they pretty near burned a hole in my shirt.

Everything else went all right, though. And the Club was fine, too. Miss Peckham got so interested in the Club and going around to the colored people and taking them medicine when they were sick and giving them Bibles and Sunday School cards and telling them stories about Jesus and Moses, she told her sister in Liberia she wasn't coming for a while.

And then one day she got a letter on the launch and she hurried to me with her face lit up like she'd just found a sack of gold dollars.

"It is from Mr. Pell that I met on the airplane," she said. "I wrote him of our labors here. And now God is bringing him on the launch next week to open a new mission at the mines. He says he will stop at Yembasi and will speak to our black children. I would not have dared to hope for such a priceless blessing. For I heard on the airplane that Mr. Pell is one of the Lord's great speakers in Africa. This will truly be a happy day."

In a week or so Mr. Pell came up on the launch. He was a awful solemn man, wearing black-rimmed glasses and bald as one of them big toadstools that grow in the jungle.

But the one thing you noticed right away was his teeth. They were all false, but they were the fanciest false teeth I ever saw, so smooth and shiny they looked like they were cut out of white marble. They must have cost plenty.

A couple of houseboys came with him, carrying his bags. He shook my hand and when he talked kind of boomed like it was thundering, the way I seen judges do when they're speaking to a court full of people, though there wasn't anybody but us around.

"I come from South Dakota," he rumbled like the thunder. "The land of the Sioux. I worked among the Red Men for many rewarding years. And then He called me over here to labor among these forgotten sons of Ham. I speak the local African tongue."

We had supper and went over to the clubhouse and took seats up on the platform. There was a good crowd, like always.

Mr. Pell turned to me and Miss Peckham. "I will give them my favorite talk," he boomed again. "It is about the sin of idleness. The black people are always fascinated by this message that I bring them. They know as well as ourselves that Satan finds work for idle hands to do."

He stopped rumbling now and began to speak the funny kind of African language they talked there, that was one minute like a hen clucking to her chickens and the next like when you breathe out doing setting-up exercises. Course I didn't understand a word.

He went on and on talking, and I was sure getting wore out. I took my watch and checked him. It was a hour and a half since he started and he didn't show a sign of stopping. He was like a preacher back home in Black Spring that if the undertaker found out he was going to preach a funeral sermon, the undertaker'd charge ten dollars extra, he'd be speaking so long.

But it was a funny thing, those black men just couldn't take their eyes off him. I never saw them listen to anybody like that before. Generally a lot of them got restless, just the way white people do. But this time they

188

watched him like a bird does a snake that's got it charmed.

He stopped finally and it was so quiet I could hear my watch ticking.

He saw all the faces turned toward him and he wiped his bald head a couple of times with a handkerchief and looked at me very proud.

"I am happy that God has given me the power to hold these black men with my message," he boomed like the thunder again.

We were getting ready to leave when one of the black people come up to him, a tall fellow wearing a hyena skin and with his body all covered with scars, not from tattooing but from fighting. But he was all smiles now.

"O Master, we have heard your houseboys tell of your wonderful teeth that you take out each night and put in a glass," he said. "We have been watching these teeth all the time you have been speaking. Please will you take them out and put them in a glass so that we can see these wonderful teeth also?"

Lucky just then Miss Peckham came up and said something to Mr. Pell so he didn't hear the black man. I guess if he had it'd been like setting off a box of dynamite behind a herd of bulls.

Mr. Pell was a kind of funny fellow. But he was all right. A little while after he was gone he sent us a old moving-picture machine, and some religious pictures for it. But there was some regular movies, too, and some of them was Westerns. And we'd hook the machine to the dynamo on the launch when it was laying up for the night, and have a show.

The black people loved the Westerns like the Arabs, and they'd holler their heads off when the cowboys and soldiers was fighting the Indians. And me and Louie'd put on our Western clothes and do the lassooing and rope tricks like we did with the Wheel. All the black people wanted cowboy suits like ours. But we just had old uniforms and Army dungarees.

Like Suleiman said, though, seeing American things made the black people want to buy them, so when they couldn't get the cowboy suits they took the Army things. So now all the men in Yembasi, instead of being pretty near naked, looked like they were in the Army when you didn't have a good supply sergeant. Because none of the clothes fit.

We sold out the clothes a couple of times, and when Suleiman came up to look things over he said I was getting along fine. And he said if I kept on the way I was doing, he'd make me a partner.

Miss Peckham got along good, too. She went around more and more, giving the black families things to eat, and helping the women when they had babies, and nursing the old people when they were sick. She helped them a lot and they sure liked her.

And then one day a lot of boxes of stuff come from Fall River, so many they pretty near filled up the launch. Louie and me opened them up and they were full of things to eat, canned beans and canned tomatoes, but mostly cans of peanut butter. It seems a fellow named Cutter that'd been a wholesale grocer in Fall River was going out of business, and sent the things to Miss Peckham before he quit.

When she came over and saw the boxes Miss Peckham was awful happy. "This Mr. Cutter is a wonderful man," she said. "He has sent us many kind gifts, but this to feed the mouths of these poor black children is his kindest. When I return to Bab-El-Kebir I will name a bench for him in the Sunday School."

Miss Peckham was busy taking care of some sick people and so she told Louie to take charge of passing the cans around.

Well, the black people liked the beans and the tomatoes, but they just loved the peanut butter. You could see them eating it everywhere, just like it was candy.

I was over at the clubhouse with Gwani when a black man come in with his wife and a couple of children.

"He would like two cans of the golden butter, Master," Gwani said after they'd talked a minute. "He has brought the money."

"Tell him to keep his money," I said. "These cans are a present from a friend of Miss Peckham in America. This peanut butter is free."

But the black man shook his head and kept holding out a handful of coins.

Gwani listened and turned to me again. "He says you have made a mistake, Master. He says he does not wish to cheat you and Miss Peckham. He knows this golden butter is a wonderful thing and that the price must be very high. For each can the black people always pay Louie four shillings."

This was too much. I couldn't have him cheating the black people like that, so I went out and found him and we had a terrible argument. I didn't speak to him for a couple of days. But he kept begging so hard for us to be friends I finally broke down.

"I'll forget it now," I said. "But it's the last time. If it happens once more you can go back to Bab-El-Kebir. You and me'll be through."

And he took my hands and swore he'd never cheat anybody again as long as he lived.

It was sure interesting living there. Wasn't a day you didn't find something new. Miss Peckham was always in the Club late in the afternoon and Aziza and me used to go over to find out if she needed anything, and then just before sunset we'd walk along the river to see the hippopotamus playing and the birds coming down to the palm trees and the big reeds for the night.

It wasn't safe, because there were always crocodiles waiting to grab you, and you didn't know what was in the tall grass, a snake, or a buffalo waiting to charge you. He's the worst game in Africa. But it was awful pretty, and Aziza after living out in the desert all her life was crazy about the water.

She'd take off her sandals and put her pretty feet in the river and little stars'd come in her eyes, and she'd sing a Arab song about living in a land full of brooks and fountains. It was a song wrote by a Arab poet, she said. I wrote a poem about the river one day, too. I kept it for a couple of months. But it was ate by the ants.

We'd been out by the river one day, when I saw a little mouse deer that'd been hurt someway so it could hardly walk. I went after it to find out if I could fix up its leg. I'm pretty good with animals, being a cowboy, and I hate to see anything suffer.

It was faster than I figured, but I finally caught it, and I saw it was bleeding bad where it'd been bit by something in the foot. They're pretty little things, these mouse deer, just like a regular deer only not as big as a small dog even. This one looked at me kind of sad when I began working on its foot, and let me fix it without any fuss, like it knew I was helping.

"It is a beautiful deer, Yance," Aziza said. "I would like to take it back to the store and keep it for a pet."

She always talked English now. It was pretty to hear her talk, kind of stiff like foreign people. And then she'd laugh like the Japanese bells whenever she'd make a mistake.

I cleaned up the deer's leg and tied it with a handkerchief and took it under my arm and we started back. It was later than I'd figured, and before we knew it the sun set and it was night. I wasn't feeling too happy, having Aziza there with me. Because I didn't have my gun or a flashlight, either. And without them a riverbank in Africa ain't a good place to be.

I went along careful, making her walk close to me, kind of feeling the way and hoping we wouldn't step on a crocodile. There were heavy clouds over us, getting ready to rain the way it did every day. And it was black as pitch.

All of a sudden I felt Aziza go all tight. She stopped and listened. "Something is following us, Yance," she said.

I stopped and listened, too. Because like I said, she could hear and see wonderful, better than me, even if I ain't so bad myself.

I could make out a kind of faint "Pat! Pat!" coming through the grass. And then the little deer in my arms started shivering.

"It's something big," I said. "And it ain't a buffalo, because the deer wouldn't be scared. Maybe it's a leopard or a lion."

193

We went on a little way, always hearing that "Pat! Pat!" coming after us. It was a little brighter for a minute now with some stars shining through the clouds. And then all of a sudden back in the grass, I saw two red balls that were like if you pulled a couple of hot coals out of a fire. They were the eyes of a leopard looked big as a horse that was coming after us, closer and closer. He was so near I could have counted the spots on him. And I could see he was winding up the way those big cats do, getting ready to spring.

Well, I didn't have a gun. And there wasn't even a stick around I could use to try to beat him off. So I done the way I did out in Texas once when a mountain lion was following me. I gave a big jump at him and let out a Indian yell they must have heard down in Joburg. And the leopard turned and run like a dog with a tin can tied to his tail. The big cats are funny like that, they say. You never can tell what they're going to do.

We come back all right with the deer. And we got him well, and he made a cute pet and followed Aziza everywhere, like the goat done in Bab-El-Kebir.

Like I said, it was interesting.

CHAPTER SEVENTEEN

I GUESS EVERYTHING would have been all right if it hadn't been for Omambe, the chief's son.

Besides my not letting him take things from the store without paying, he got mad at me on account of the watch.

I had a watch I'd brought with me from the States, one of those cheap pocket watches used to sell for a dollar 'way back, but now cost two-ninety-eight.

It stopped running and I tried to fix it, because I needed a watch bad and you couldn't get any there. But it was broke for good so I gave it to a old colored man worked around the store. The old fellow used to wear it on a string around his chest whenever he dressed up, and he was prouder of that busted watch than I was in the rodeo when I almost broke the record for roping a calf.

I noticed Omambe looking at me meaner than ever after that, and I wondered why. And come to find out, he was mad at me for giving the watch to the old man. He figured I'd ought to have give it to him instead, so he could put it on the chain with the keys.

It was like one of them Pekinese dogs the lady had that kept the boardinghouse where I stayed in Houston. He lived on birds' tongues, pretty near, but if he was looking out the window and seen you giving a piece of dry bread to a poor old dog used to hang around there, he'd wait till next night when you were right in the middle of eating chicken or something special, and then he'd run up and bite you in the leg so hard it felt like he'd bit through the bone.

But what started the bad trouble was the athletics. Everybody that came along, the engineer, and Mr. Pell, and Miss Peckham's sister in Liberia all said that athletics were wonderful for civilizing the black people. And I was trying to figure out what we'd do, when one day Louie and me are unpacking some crates of surplus, and sure enough if there ain't a lot of baseballs and bats and things, going to some PX, I guess, that the poor soldiers never got in time.

That was just what I'd been looking for, and right away we went out in back of the Club, and cut down the high grass—more funny kind of snakes come out of it than you ever saw in your life—and we made some bases and marked out a batter's and a pitcher's box, and before you knew it, we had a beautiful diamond.

Well, seemed like there were two big clans in the village, just like the Indians out West have the Bear and the Wolf clans, only here they were the Leopards and the Hyenas. I made each of them pick a team and showed them how to play, and in no time we had a game going. Though we had to stop for a little while when a bunch of elephants came down the river from somewhere and tramped around pulling up palm trees, and breaking up the benches we'd fixed so people could watch.

Those black fellows took to baseball like they'd been born with a glove on their hands, especially the Hyenas. I didn't know, but the Hyenas were kind of lower class than the Leopards. The chiefs came from the Leopard clan and at first the Hyenas didn't want to beat them. But I kept telling them that sure wasn't any way to play baseball and they ought to get out there and play with everything they've got.

So then they really played and they beat the spots off the Leopards. And the Leopards were pretty mad.

The chief's son hadn't played the first couple of days. I guess he was too proud. But when he saw the Leopards getting whipped all the time, I guess he figured he ought to do something, so one afternoon when the Leopards were losing again he said he wanted to get in the game. And course he wanted to be the pitcher.

Well, the Leopards were in bad shape and the Hyenas were hitting them pretty hard, and the score was 5 to 0 or something like that, when this Omambe steps in the pitcher's box.

He winds up and throws the first ball and I didn't need to see any more to know he was terrible. He was the worst player of all. I figured the Hyenas would knock him all around the lot. But funny thing, they wouldn't touch a ball he sent over. They just struck right out.

It happened this way for two innings without a bat even scraping a ball cover, and this Omambe just stood there, looking awful smart.

I was umpiring and I got all upset, because I like to see things go right.

"What's the matter with them?" I said to Louie that was out there with me, so he's handy. "What's happened to all them good hitters?"

"He's the chief's son," Louie answered. "They don't want to get in trouble."

"The chief's son ain't God Almighty," I said. "We don't do like that with baseball in the States."

I left Louie to do the umpiring and came down to talk to the fellow at bat that's the captain of the Hyenas, a skinny fellow as tall as Gwani, just wearing a pair of khaki shorts, and tattooed all over his body with blue dots so he looks like one of them China salt cellars.

"You go ahead and hit the ball," I said. "In a ball game the chief's son ain't no different than anybody else. In the States everybody's the same in a game even if it's the President. You got to play to win."

I got him persuaded and next ball comes over, crack! he knocked it out toward the swamp along the river where the left fielder had to argue about a ball with the crocodiles, and course it was a home run.

The next Hyenas up were still kind of scared, even after I talked to them, and they didn't hit as hard as the captain, but they got the bases full with no outs. And the chief's son was getting awful nervous. And then a Hyena that was a kind of assistant captain, a little ratty black fellow, awful smart, come up and began swinging his bat.

I knew he wouldn't be scared of anything. "Here's your chance," I said. "Hit hard and bring them three men on bases in."

Well, the ball comes over and it was awful wild, way off the plate, because like I said, the chief's son had got awful nervous. But this little ratty fellow almost run after it and hit it someway and knocked it so far they never did find it. All the men come running home and course after that nobody was afraid any more, and everybody that went up to the plate hit the ball out of sight. There were so many runs I couldn't count them.

The chief's son kept getting wilder and wilder, and finally he gave some terrible kind of curse and threw his glove and the ball on the ground and stomped off the field. And course the game's over.

That night I was sound asleep when I heard somebody talking to me. I woke up all of a sudden and saw Aziza sitting up in bed in her nightgown, shaking my arm, all excited.

"I smell smoke, Yance," she said. "I think the store is on fire."

I smelled the smoke in a minute, too, and I jumped out of bed. Just then flames started shooting up from a corner of the porch. Aziza and me grabbed buckets and I called Louie and Gwani. And they come right behind us with pans and things and we got water on the fire in a hurry. When the smoke died down, we saw where some dry branches had been piled up under the porch floor. And it didn't take us long to figure out who done it.

Louie was awful mad. He come to me a few days later with some kind of funny powder looked like flour.

"I asked one of the black men on the launch to buy this for me, Joe," he said. "He got it from a witch doctor up the river. I will have one of the wives of the chief's son put this in his meat when he eats. It will not kill him. It will only make him very sick with the fever for a month. And no one will ever know."

Course I didn't let him. But when I get to thinking of all the things that happened afterward I sure ought to have let him use something even worse.

I got the baseball games patched up by giving the Leopards a lot of canned goods from the store, and we picked the teams a different way so the Leopards and the Hyenas'd be mixed up, and the chief's son didn't play any more. And the baseball started again, better than ever.

I guess word about the trouble got around, and they heard about it down at Kimali, where the District Commissioner was, and one day I see a big launch flying the British flag come up to the dock, so white and shiny you could eat ice cream off the deck. I knew it was the District Commissioner's launch. And in a minute the Commissioner himself came down the gangplank, with a couple of black soldiers in fancy uniform, and he walked over to the store.

He was a tall, kind of sandy Englishman with a little dude mustache, like the Englishmen I seen playing tennis lots of places in North Africa. He's a stiff fellow, the same kind as that American Consul from Algiers, and talked awful funny the way all those fancy Englishmen do, like a cabdriver out in San Antonio had a operation on his throat and it didn't heal up right.

"I am on my regular tour, Mr. Cullum," he said. "I have heard about your difficulties with the chief's son and I thought perhaps it would be well if I dropped in for a chat."

He looked at the wrist watch he was wearing. "We have a very delicate situation here in the Yembasi area, with the opening of the mines and all the newcomers they attract. The black people do not like the Arabs, and both the black people and the Arabs do not like the Hindus. There are some families of both races in Yembasi itself, as you know, and many others in the surrounding territory. There is, moreover, much agitation from other powers I need not name who would profit if they could stir up trouble. The slightest spark can set off a conflagration. The son of this chief is what I believe you call in America a badly spoiled egg. For the sake of your country and mine I will ask you to please be very careful."

He looked at the watch again and I got to see it close. It was one of that fancy kind you never have to wind, just works by your moving around. I'd have sure liked to own it, because I was missing a watch bad. And then he sat down and stayed a while talking like a detective, asking me a lot of questions, where I come from, and about Aziza and Louie and Suleiman.

But I didn't mind. I could see he was trying to be sociable, though he ain't used to it. And he took a Scotch and soda all them Englishmen drink, and then the two black men in uniform held the screen door open for him, and he walked over to the dock. And a minute later he was going up the river.

I figure Englishmen are all right. I knowed some English soldiers in North Africa that was pretty near as good as Americans. They sure like meat.

He's been gone a couple of hours when Louie came in

where I'm working over some papers at the desk I have in the store, and put something down in front of me.

"Here's a watch for you, Joe," he said.

I looked and I saw it's the fancy watch that belonged to the District Commissioner.

I got a bad shock and told him it was a terrible thing and we had another big argument. I asked him why he did it.

He looked kind of hurt. "You needed a watch, Joe. And the Commissioner can get another without any trouble. When you need something, I, Louie, will get it for you. Even when you do not ask."

I asked him how he'd got hold of it, because I'd seen it was buckled tight to the Commissioner's wrist.

He looked real proud. "This was nothing, Joe," he said. "I have told you many times I was the best pickpocket in Bab-El-Kebir. Mr. Dumont there will tell you the same. When the Commissioner was sitting drinking the whisky, I put some ants on the table. And when he put down the glass, the ants crawled onto his wrist and under the watch band. He took off the watch to scratch his wrist, and it was then that I picked it up. . . . I wish you would not send it back. It is a beautiful watch, Joe."

I was awful mad. But course he'd done it for me and he was so sure he'd acted right I finally told him I'd forget it this one more time. But it was his last chance. If anything like it happened again, he'd have to pack up his things and go.

I sent the watch to the Commissioner right away with a letter I wrote on fancy paper that Miss Peckham gave me saying he'd forgot it some way. And he wrote a letter back saying he was awful sorry he'd caused me the trouble.

Like I said, most of them Englishmen are nice, even if they don't talk right. I stayed in a camp outside of London a week, and went around seeing things. And I met some nice people. And a English fellow that was a big Lord, the king's brother or something, came to the camp to say how glad the English was to see us, and I shook hands and talked to him a minute, and I didn't say a word about us beating the English back there in 1776.

That London is a good town. I learned more there and in the jail in the skyscraper with the Legion fellows than almost anywhere I been.

Well, things went along wonderful for a while. The chief's son didn't play baseball any more, but everybody else played all the time. I never seen people so crazy about anything. It was the same way a GI told me it was with the Japs in Japan.

We were just about to start playing one day when Miss Peckham came up to where I was talking to some of the black people.

"I have been so interested in the games, Mr. Cullum," she said. "My parents never took me to baseball games in America and of course as I was a girl I could not play myself. Though once I was visiting at the home of a schoolmate and her brother who played on the school team looked at my arm and said I would make a very good pitcher. I have been wondering if there was any way in which I could help the players."

"Maybe you could keep score," I said.

She looked kind of thoughtful. "My uncle was the president of a bank in Fall River," she answered. "Though I never called on him there perhaps being his niece I would be competent with figures."

I gave her a pencil and pad and showed her how to mark things each inning.

In the middle of the game Gwani came for me and I had to go over to the store, leaving Gwani to do the umpiring. When I got back I saw a lot of the black people around Miss Peckham, arguing awful loud.

I hurried to them.

Miss Peckham looked up from the pad she was holding. Her face was worried. "They say I have put down runs where I should have put outs and where there were runs I have marked them as errors," she said. "Perhaps if you have a book on baseball I could study it before I keep the score again."

Before long we sold all the baseballs and bats we had, and I wrote Suleiman to send off for more. And then they came, and this time there were too many. So I began taking them around to the other beehive villages that weren't far away. And course I had to show them how to play.

And they liked it just the same as the people in Yembasi. And they'd have fights and get mad at the umpires, just like they did back home in Black Spring.

Whenever I could I used to take Aziza out in a little boat I'd fixed up with a gas engine. Like I said, she loved the water so. We'd go along the river a short way, and then maybe we'd turn into a creek with the banks so close together and the trees and vines so thick all around you'd think you'd never find your way out again in a hundred years.

And then all of a sudden you'd come into a open space, and you'd see beautiful long-legged birds wading in the water and a family of deer on the shore drinking. And you knew you were the first white person that'd ever been there. And it was like you were in the Garden of Eden.

We came to a place like that one day when we were taking the afternoon off, and it was so beautiful we stopped the boat and climbed out on the bank. A couple of big antelope with long horns were under a palm tree, but they weren't scared at all. They just stood watching us like they'd never seen a man before.

We started walking, and it was like a park, with little trees everywhere and the grass all cut pretty and smooth between so it was just like a lawn. Course it was the wild animals that kept it that way. And then we saw what they call gazelles, and a flock of ostriches kicking up dust like a cattle stampede out in Texas.

Aziza ran across the grass ahead of me, picking up some flowers that were growing under the trees, and then running back and showing them to me and putting them in her hair. She'd been getting gayer and gayer ever since we left Bab-El-Kebir. And then she put flowers all over my hair, too, so I looked like one of those Hawaiians.

And then we sat down under a low tree, kind of spread out like a umbrella, and she sang a couple of Arab songs. She lay close to me and looked up through the tree branches, where the little birds were flying like jewels.

"I think we are in Paradise," she said.

A couple of minutes later I heard a funny kind of barking in the distance. And I looked out and I seen a lot of animals running toward us. At first I thought they were hyenas, they were about the same size, and had the same kind of stripes. And then they came a little closer and I didn't have to look any more.

I pulled Aziza to her feet. "It's wild dogs," I said. "Climb up in the tree."

I boosted her onto a bough and climbed up after her. And a minute later the dogs were all around the trunk, barking and snarling and jumping up in the air, trying to get at us. There were about thirty or forty of them, I guess, and they were horrible-looking, with teeth twice as big as wolves and their jaws opening and shutting with a noise like a lot of rat traps springing.

Well, it sure wasn't pretty looking down at all those teeth snapping, especially when I'd heard that next to the buffalo they were the worst game in Africa. They could kill a lion.

In a couple of minutes there's more barking, and another bunch of dogs came up, and I was hoping they'd start a fight with the first. But they were part of the same pack, I guess, because they knew the other dogs, and come over and joined up with them, and started jumping and scratching at the tree trunk like they were cats. Some of them were good jumpers, too, and one of them got awful close to Aziza's dress. And I made her climb higher in the tree. Though she couldn't go far. The tree wasn't much bigger than the olive trees I seen all over North Africa.

I didn't know what we were going to do. I'd heard plenty about the dogs trapping people, and keeping them up in a tree till they died. Nobody knew where we were, and I didn't know how long it would take before Gwani and the black people could find us in that wild country. And after a couple of days up in that tree, even if nothing else got us, with all the ants and mosquitos and snakes around, there wouldn't be much of us left. Course I could have shot a few of the dogs, but I didn't have enough bullets to do any good.

Aziza was awful brave. She just stayed there by me, looking down at those wild things out of her big brown eyes as quiet as if she was back at the house, studying her English book. It was the same way little Zuleima did that time in the pickup when the brakes wouldn't hold. Those Arab girls are sure wonderful.

"I heard the storyteller at Bab-El-Kebir tell of an Arab who was up in a tree surrounded by wild boars," she said. "And he happened to say a magic word, and the boars all ran away."

"We could sure use a word like that right now," I told her.

Well, the dogs kept snapping and jumping a couple of hours, I guess, and then they just settled down to wait. They got so still laying there you'd have swore to look at them they were just a bunch of nice Airedales or something on a place in the States where they breed dogs for rich people.

We stayed up in the tree with the dogs under us till the sun was beginning to drop 'way down in the sky and I was sure getting worried. I saw some big snake holes right under the tree, and soon as it got dark I knew the snakes would start coming out. And I knew there'd be plenty of leopards the same way. They'd been killing the black people bad lately. And leopards wasn't like the dogs. The leopards could climb trees.

The dogs began getting hungry now, I guess, and they got up and began barking and jumping worse than ever, coming so high in the tree it looked like we wouldn't need to wait for the leopards. When all of a sudden there's a cloud of dust in the distance. The cloud keeps moving toward us, and I make out it's a big herd of antelope. And the dogs saw the herd the same time, too. Course the antelope were better eating for the dogs than us. So the dogs took off across the grass after them, and we climbed down out of the tree, and hurried back to the boat and the store.

Animals are sure like people, ain't they? Next morning I passed the chief's son, and this time he was all smiling and polite. And I couldn't help thinking it was just like the dogs when they were laying under the tree looking so gentle and quiet, when all the time they were really waiting to tear us to pieces. It was the same way with the fellow in the rodeo that stole the shirts.

Every time I seen the chief's son after that I thought of the dogs and it gave me the shivers. I wished plenty of times he'd stop coming to the store because I always had to watch him close so he wouldn't hide a snake or a poison lizard someplace. I'd heard plenty about the queer things people like him did in that country.

Once after he left I opened a drawer and a big scorpion that would have give me a terrible sting just missed me. Course it might have crawled in there by itself. I never did know.

But I didn't bother thinking about him if I could help it. With the launch coming in every day bringing the supplies Suleiman sent, and taking care of the customers and the people staying overnight, and looking after the baseball games and the Club, I sure didn't have no time to kill, the way they say.

The store kept going fine, and Suleiman kept writing how pleased he was the way I was doing. Like I told you, I'm a good business man, having owned the grocery and things like that, and I always kept on thinking how I could make things better.

I thought plenty of times about starting up the laundry here, because I knew it'd be a big success. Every day you could see the black women trying to wash their clothes in the river and then the crocodiles would come after them and pretty often they'd catch somebody. But I couldn't have the laundry because there wasn't any electricity to run the machinery.

And then I thought about the Orange Drink. We'd done awful good with that when we had the Wheel and I saw the black people liked candy and sweet things even more than the Arabs. So I wrote a letter to the office of the big American company in Casablanca the Frenchman that handled the drink in Marrakeesh had told me about, and asked if we could get it in Yembasi.

And then one day the launch stopped at the dock, and I saw a man get out, and right away I could tell this fellow was a American, even if he was wearing a white helmet and white shorts like a Englishman.

He walked into the store and put out his hand quick.

"Ziegler's the name," he said, talking kind of like a machine gun. "B. J. Ziegler. Good old German name. St. Louis, Missouri. Trans-Africa Enterprises. Just taken over our new territory out of Accra. They forwarded your letter about Orange Drink that you sent to Casa. Anything we can do, just count on B.J."

I told him I'd like to get the Orange Drink at the store as soon as I could.

He put a big cigar in his mouth and gave me one, too. "You'll have it," he said. "Next Tuesday on the launch. Any place in Africa can have it now. I'm on my way to the mines up river to arrange their supply. This soft-drink business is spreading so fast we've had to open up three new bottling plants in four months. One in Joburg, one at Leopoldville in the Congo, and one at Lagos in Nigeria. Soft drinks are the biggest thing in Africa since the Kimberley gold strike. And Orange Drink is outselling its competitors three to one. Have another cigar."

He stayed for supper like people generally did, rattling off his words like the marines firing the day we landed on the beach in North Africa, and I tell you he was smart. That French fellow in Marrakeesh was mighty bright, too. I guess they wouldn't let them handle the drink if they weren't smart people.

"You've got a wonderful place here," he said. "Wonderful chance to grow. On a river. That's what made St. Louis and New Orleans. Chicago, too. On a lake. Same thing."

He kept the cigar rolling in his mouth like a pinwheel. "I'd like to see you expand. And Trans-Africa Enterprises is the company to help you. We handle drugs, furniture, electrical goods, machinery, automobiles. Everything the white man needs in Africa. That's our motto. I'd like to see you have a store all your own. When you're doing well, keep progressing. A young man like you can't afford to stand still."

I told him about how I'd like to start the laundry, but we didn't have any electricity.

"Can fix you up with that, too," he said. "Sell you a

portable power plant for a thousand dollars. Used a little, but shipshape. Sell electricity to your Arab friend, too. Fine investment. Then someday you can open your own place up the river. You'd better order that power plant while I'm here. Or when I get back to Accra it'll be gone."

I talked it over with Louie and Aziza and Miss Peckham that night. And the more I talked and thought about it, the more I liked the idea. Suleiman had told me any time I wanted to start the laundry, it was all right with him. And I knew he'd take the electricity, because I'd heard him say he wished he could get it in the store.

Even without the laundry, the power plant'd be a wonderful thing. It was too good a chance to miss. So I told Mr. Ziegler I'd do it. I gave him three hundred dollars in cash that I had and signed a paper for the rest.

I got the Orange Drink next week, and a letter from Mr. Ziegler saying that it'd be a little while before the electric plant come. He found out the plant was at Joburg, and not at Accra the way he figured.

He'd got me thinking, though, with that about not standing still. And when the Orange Drink came, and I saw the black people buying it fast, I started figuring if there was something to eat that would go with it good. And then I remembered how the hamburgers and hot dogs went so quick at the laundry opening.

We had plenty of meat that came up on the launch, and some of the black people had cattle besides. So I went to a black man that was a good carpenter and got him to make me a hamburger stand with wheels so you could move it around, and then me and Aziza painted it up all pretty with trees and lions and leopards and monkeys and things that were right for Africa. And I got another fellow that made war spears to make me a hamburger grill.

And then I showed the cook how to make hamburgers and franks, the way I did the Arabs in Bab-El-Kebir, and I told Gwani to take the stand down to the dock where the black men's canoes came in.

I've had plenty of good ideas, but that hamburger stand was sure one of the best. Them colored fellows'd come out of the canoes all hot and tired and hungry. And every one of them would buy a hamburger and take a Orange Drink. And then whenever there was a game going on the baseball diamond, I'd tell Gwani to take the stand over, and the people there'd buy plenty of them, too.

Course sometimes a bunch of monkeys'd come down from the trees and grab them all and run. And one afternoon when a game was going, a lion came down—I guess his nose got the hamburger smell—and he ate up all the burgers and kind of busted up the stand before anybody could get spears or a gun. But we got it fixed in a hurry.

Suleiman came up a few days after and he figured out our profits. And he said he was sure glad he'd met me, and it wouldn't be long now before he made me a partner.

The Club was going fine, too. Me and Miss Peckham kept fixing it up, making it nicer all the time. But you had to be careful. Because sometimes things happened a way you didn't figure.

Like that about Easter.

Miss Peckham told me Easter was coming pretty soon, and how she wished she could do something about it. And I got to thinking about Easter once in Black Spring when some of the rich people had a pet show for everybody. And I thought it'd be nice if we'd have a pet show here in Yembasi, with prizes for the best lion or leopard cub or deer. And maybe we'd get the people started having pets like me and Aziza, the way everybody does in the States.

Miss Peckham thought it was a fine idea, so we decided on the prizes and things, and said we'd have the show in the Club on Easter Day. And in a few days everywhere you'd go in the village you'd see the black people with a monkey or a gazelle maybe they'd begun taking care of for the show.

And then I found out from Gwani they didn't understand the way it was at all. They weren't raising the animals for pets, but to eat. They couldn't figure what else anybody would do it for.

So I paid everybody to let the animals go and called off the show.

Things were always happening in the store, too. A bunch of transfer pictures came in the stock and I was surprised to see the black men buy them so fast we sold out in a day. They pasted them all over their bodies. There were travel scenes from everywhere, and it was kind of funny meeting a big black fellow all covered with pictures of the castle where the Queen of England lives, and girls in bathing suits under a palm tree saying "Come to Florida."

I was walking over from the village maybe a week after when I see a big crowd of the black people in front of the store, and then I see they're arguing with Louie.

I could tell they were awful mad, and I hurried up and asked Louie what was the matter.

Louie looked worried. "I sold them the transfer pictures to use instead of tattooing," he said. "And now they have come and are asking for their money back. I did not tell them the pictures would come off."

The black people carried on pretty bad for a while, hollering and yelling at Louie like they were going to kill him, but I finally fixed things up and they went back to the village.

I was telling Louie what I thought, when I found out he'd been cheating them other ways besides. So I told him I couldn't stand it any longer and he'd have to leave on the launch going down river next day.

The boat came in that night, and he told the Englishman that ran it he'd be taking the trip in the morning.

I didn't say anything to Miss Peckham about how he was going back to Bab-El-Kebir, because I didn't want her to know the reason. Or I didn't tell Aziza either. I just said he had to go down where Suleiman was for a few days to see about some things for the store.

We all had supper together. Aziza and Miss Peckham were especially gay that night, telling him all kinds of things to bring back. But Louie and me just stayed at the table there looking miserable.

And then in the morning I walked down with him to the dock where the boat was getting ready to leave, and he took his bundle and went aboard.

The motor started up and he sat on a coil of rope, all bent over, looking like a monkey I seen in the animal pound in Houston once, that'd lost his master.

The boat was just pulling out when I couldn't stand it any longer.

"Come back, Louie!" I shouted.

And he gave a big jump and landed on the dock and throwed his arms around me.

He undid his bundle and lifted out a little black box he always took especial care of, and he gave it to me, and dropped to his knees. And the tears began streaming down his face like when he told the Arabs the number of beans in the jar.

"This is the box where I keep every shilling of my money, Joe," he sobbed. "I swear this by my mother and father. You count it every week. If it has only the money you pay me then you will know I am honest. But if you find more, then I have cheated again and I will ask you to tie me to a tree by the river and let the leopards and the crocodiles eat me."

I didn't want to do it, but every payday he made me take the box and count the money like he said. And I couldn't find a penny wrong.

CHAPTER EIGHTEEN

Aziza and me got along fine, but once in a while things got tangled up pretty bad because I was a American and she was a Arab. She worried a lot because we were so different.

One night Miss Peckham gave me some magazines that had just come from the States. There was a piece in one of them about Texas with a whole page of pictures, a street in a little place looked kind of like Black Spring and a rodeo and people on ranches. I cut the pictures out and put them up on the wall.

I noticed Aziza was awful quiet that night, and the next few days I saw her going around the house awful sad, looking just the way she did in the laundry when she found out she'd have to marry the pig-eyed man, only now you could tell by the way she was holding her face and lips all tight she was keeping herself from crying.

I tried to find out what was the matter, but she wouldn't say anything.

And then after supper I was looking through another magazine, full of pictures of pretty girls and things, when she came out of the kitchen and stood in front of my chair.

She stayed there a minute, kind of quivering. "I am ready for you to divorce me, Yance," she said.

I was so surprised I could hardly answer. "You sick or something, Aziza?" I asked her finally. "You just ain't talking right."

She spoke again, so low if you hadn't seen her lips moving a little you'd hardly know she was talking. "I have thought often you might wish to go home and marry one of your own people," she told me. "All the time I have seen you reading these books with beautiful girls and I knew it was because they reminded you of the girls of your country and perhaps of a girl that you loved. And four days ago you put this picture on the wall and then I knew it was true."

I told her I couldn't understand a word she was saying.

She led me over to where I'd pinned up the photographs of Texas I'd cut out from the magazine.

"I saw you looking at her picture and smiling all the time," she said. "And then I knew this was the girl you really love and wish to marry instead of me."

She showed me a big picture in the middle. It was a cowgirl riding a horse in a rodeo.

I busted out laughing and I drew her close to me and told her I'd never seen the girl in my life. All I was interested in was the horse.

And course in a few minutes she was laughing like me.

Like I said, everything would have been all right if it hadn't been for the chief's son.

I was in the store one day and Miss Peckham came in on her way to the Club, wearing the black dress and black hat she always had on, even though it was so hot. She waited in front of the counter a minute, and I could see she was kind of embarrassed. She looked like the music teacher in Black Spring when she stopped at our house once when they were collecting money for a new organ in the church, and you could see she just hated to ask.

"I would like to talk to you about these poor black women among whom I have been working, Mr. Cullum," she said. "You have seen them standing so pitifully outside the windows of the Club on the night the motion picture is shown, trying vainly to look inside. It has made tears come to my eyes many times. They ask so little, these poor women. Their sad condition is even worse than the Mohammedan women of Bab-El-Kebir. A few days ago you showed a film sent by Mr. Pell of the last days of Rome with a great chariot race. It was a beautiful picture, showing how the Romans were punished for their iniquities. I wished then that the women might have been present, for its moral tone was very high. But alas, this was not possible."

She dabbed her face kind of nervous again with a fancy little handkerchief. "This morning, the fourth wife of the chief's son, the tall one I call Bathsheeba, came to me and told me about this film and others which they had not seen but of which they had heard from the men of the village. She asked if the young chief's wives and the other women could in the future attend the showings. I told her I did not have the authority, that this property where the Club stands belongs to Mr. Suleiman and I must make the request of you. Do you think their request might be granted? If it could I think it would please our Lord greatly. And perhaps Mr. Pell might even send us the film with the chariot race and the Fall of Rome again."

Well, I thought it over that night. I figured the old chief and the other men might not like having the women, being so strict the way they were about not allowing any of them around, but it sure didn't seem right not to let them come to a moving picture. And I got to thinking about the U.S. consul again and the way people do in America, and we sure let women go to a picture show.

So next morning when Miss Peckham came in to breakfast with Aziza and me and Louie, I told her she could tell them to come.

Her face shone like gold the way the trees across the river did at sunup. She left the table and went to her room and came back all ready to go out.

"I will let Bathsheeba know at once," she said. "This will make the poor women of Yembasi very happy. And it will make all my dear friends of the Mission in Fall River very happy, too."

Well, we had another picture in a couple of nights, and just before it started Miss Peckham came marching in all smiling, but stiff and straight like a little general, with maybe thirty or forty black women behind her. They all took seats on the long benches.

The old chief and the black men were all sitting there,

watching, and I held my breath ready for anything. But the chief and the others didn't move or make a sound. They just looked like they were paralyzed. And I started the show fast. And then they got interested in the screen, I guess. And nothing happened at all.

It was a good show, told about a poor girl in New York that worked in a factory and wanted to get married, and went up North in Canada and fell in love with a fellow and was going to marry him. But he turned out to be a escaped murderer that was going to kill her, and a man from the Northwest Mounted came along and saved her, and married her instead.

And then the show ended, and Miss Peckham marched the women out again.

The chief's son hadn't been at the movie that night. If he had, I guess things would have been different because I heard he blew up like a boiler explosion when they told him. He had sixty wives, I found out. Most of them weren't really wives at all, they just worked out in the fields for him or pounded meal till long after dark.

I heard he wanted to do something awful to his wives to keep them from going to the show again, but his father wouldn't let him because he'd get in trouble with the English police. And now the women had started coming they wouldn't stop and they come every time, especially the young chief's wives that had been talking to Miss Peckham.

I met him one night when the show was over and the women were all walking out. And I seen him looking at me mean as a coyote that's just killed a calf and you rode up and drove him away.

Well, it wasn't long afterward when I came up to where

the black people were all sitting in a circle near the chief's house, and I saw a black man walking up and down in the middle, making a speech and arguing his head off about something. And then he sat down and a couple of other fellows got up and started talking what I figured was against him, and you could tell the way they were going they'd make a politician back home giving a election speech look tongue-tied.

Louie came up then and I asked him what they were doing.

"It's what they call a palaver, Joe," he said. "All the black people in this country have palavers when they want to settle anything. Some of the people here want to plant bananas in the fields down by the river, and some of them say no, they want to raise cocoa. It's been going on for a whole day now, and Gwani says it will go on for two days more."

Louie said Gwani had told him all the black people here were wonderful what they call orators and they loved to talk. He'd seen palavers that went on for a week. I figured a palaver was about the same as the big powwows the Indians used to have out West.

Funny, ain't it, how your mind gets to going. I got to thinking about people arguing two sides of something. And I remembered about a time when I was in the fifth grade the teacher took us to hear the Black Spring High School have what they call a debate with the High School from Flat Top, that was a little town near there.

It was a fine debate. The subject was "Which did more for the human race, the horse or the cow?" Black Spring had the cow and they really won it, but two of the judges was raising horses, so they gave it to Flat Top.

Well, things had been going kind of slow at the Club, and I got to figuring that with all these black fellows liking to make speeches maybe we could have a debating society and have some good debates every once in a while.

I told Miss Peckham about it over at the Club.

She got all excited. "It is a wonderful plan," she said. "My sister often has debates at her mission in Liberia. When I was a girl in school at Fall River I had a beloved teacher, a Mr. Persons, who told me there was nothing that equaled a debate to train and sharpen the mind. I was in one debate on who was the greater general, Alexander or Napoleon, and my school won with Alexander."

Her eyes got sad. "But my parents did not let me take part again. They said they were afraid it might lead me to go on the stage."

The black men took to that debating just like they did the baseball. A couple of times a week they'd be debating all kinds of things, which was better to live in, grass or trees, and which was stronger, the lion or the elephant.

Course the women had been coming to the picture shows, so they started going to hear the men debating, too. I was talking to Miss Peckham one day and it came to me it would be a good idea, maybe, if we got the women on one side debating the men, the way they did a couple of times at the High School in Black Spring.

Miss Peckham got all happy again. "I have a splendid subject," she said. "I have just read of it in the little mission paper my sister sends me from Liberia. The men and women there debated, 'Which is better, one wife or many wives?' It was the most successful debate the mission has ever had."

I figured we couldn't find anything better, so Miss Peckham and me picked the sides, with the women of course taking the one wife. It sure stirred up plenty of excitement. When the night for the debate came around, there wasn't a empty seat in the clubhouse. Even some of the Syrians and the Hindus walked over from the other part of the village. And people were packed around the doors and the windows, trying to get a good look inside.

Miss Peckham and Aziza and Louie and me were the judges, two men and two women to make it fair. We were all sitting up on the platform with Gwani in the middle to tell us what the black people were saying. I let Louie be one of the judges because it looked like he was behaving fine.

Miss Peckham stood up and called the first speaker, the young chief's wife Bathsheeba she'd spoke about, a tall, light-skinned colored girl wearing a red cotton dress like a lot of them bought at the store, with a big blue comb in her hair.

She was a fine talker. She started out awful quiet at first, so soft you could hardly hear her, and then all of a sudden she'd switch and pace up and down and get all fierce like a lioness, and then she'd kind of beg the people with tears in her voice, like she was asking them to help save somebody who was going to be hung. You could tell right away she was the kind of woman that somewhere else would have been a woman mayor or a preacher.

After her came the first of the men, a stout fellow that was a kind of slick politician, dressed up in a blue shirt and white shorts, and all the time he just kept waving his arms like a windmill and roaring out his words like a bull.

There were two more women, both wearing dresses like Bathsheeba's, and two more men, one with a leopard skin over his shoulders and some tails around his waist, and the other with a kind of beaded skirt like the young chief wore on big days.

From the first minute anybody could see who was going to win. The women were ten times better than the men, especially with that Bathsheeba. She came in at the end like the lioness again, and her voice echoed back and forth from the walls so strong it made your whole body shake. And then the women began chanting with her, just like they were in a Holy Roller church. And then all of a sudden she gave a terrible cry, like Daniel calling on the Lord to take him out of the fiery furnace, and she threw her arms out to the women. And they began shouting and cheering. And the debate's over.

The four of us that were the judges voted right away for the women. And when Miss Peckham told the crowd, the women gave a big shout that pretty near tore down the roof. And they all crowded around Bathsheeba like people do a fellow that wins a football game. But some of the men stood around in bunches, glaring at the women terrible mad, and saying what they'd do to their wives when they got home.

The chief's son went by where I was standing at the door with Aziza and Miss Peckham. And his face was like stone and his eyes were burning like a tiger.

Things quieted down for a while after that. And then I heard the chief's son was going to take a new wife. Things with him and me had been getting worse and worse. But I thought Aziza and me ought to go to the wedding anyhow, and we took some presents from the store, the way we always did, and went on over.

First the young chief's wives did a dance, all sixty of them, some of them wrinkled old women. They had on little aprons made of shells and big feather necklaces, and their hair was made up high, like a house with four or five stories. And then the new bride came out, a young girl with her hair in eight stories, and she was wearing so many brass rings on her body you couldn't see a inch of skin hardly.

The young chief was there dressed fancier than ever. And him and the girl kind of bumped heads. And that made them married.

People can sure think of funny ways of marrying. A fellow I knew that drove a bus in Dallas put on a diving suit, and his girl and the preacher done the same thing, and they got married under water.

After the wedding of the young chief and the girl with the brass rings everybody began eating and drinking palm wine, and I took a little to show we were friends.

The old women led the new wife off to a beehive house they'd just finished the day before, and Bathsheeba and some of the other young ones walked behind. Bathsheeba passed close to Miss Peckham and gave her a nice smile.

And Miss Peckham looked awful happy, like the music teacher one time I seen her in the church in Black Spring when the preacher told the congregation they'd got fifty dollars more than they needed for the new organ.

"I think the Lord is blessing our labors," she said. "This Bathsheeba is a wonderful girl. Yesterday she told the chief's son that he could marry as many wives as he wished, but that she would no longer work like a slave, or let herself be sold like a sheep or a cow. And she said that soon many others of his wives and perhaps even this new wife will tell him the same. . . . I wish Mr. Suleiman were not a Mohammedan, and I could have a mission in Yembasi and teach the ways of Our Lord to Bathsheeba. I think she might become as dear to the mission here as Louie is to the Mission in Bab-El-Kebir."

I guess it was about a week after the wedding when I happened to be walking where the wives of the chief's son were digging in the fields, and I saw Bathsheeba standing there talking all excited to a crowd of the black women.

The wives were all listening close and every once in a while they'd say something loud, and they'd all kind of shout and chant like they did at the debate. And when she'd stop talking for a minute they'd mutter and shake their heads. There was a picture show in the Club that night and when the women went out they were all muttering the same way again.

Next morning I heard they told the chief's son they wouldn't do anything, even cook a meal, unless he agreed to treat them better.

Course he went wild and said he'd kill them and I don't know what all. But it wasn't more than a couple of weeks and he'd agreed to do what they said. But it sure made plenty of trouble.

A few days later I was out in the gasboat with Aziza a little way above the village where the river got wider and made a kind of lake, and all of a sudden I noticed the boat was filling up with water. I put down my hand and could feel there was a big crack in the bottom with the water pouring in like you turned on a fireplug.

I stuffed in some rags to try and stop it, but it didn't

help much and I knew we'd better get back to shore in a hurry. I raced the motor and we were moving fast when the engine gave a cough and stopped. I tried to get it running again but it wouldn't do anything. I knew we ought to have plenty of gas because I'd filled up that morning a couple of hours before we started out. But I looked at the tank anyway. And then I knew that somebody had been fooling with the boat. The tank was empty.

I always carried a pair of oars and I put them in the oarlocks quick. And then I picked up the bucket we used to carry little fish in and gave it to Aziza.

"Bail fast as you can," I said. "Things don't look so good."

I ain't a real rower, coming from dry country the way I do, but I sure used those oars that day. That little lake seemed as big to me as one of them Great Lakes I passed near Chicago when I came up North in the Army.

Aziza kept the bucket going like lightning, but all the time the water kept rising higher. I found a loose board I hadn't seen at the back, and put it over the hole and tried to keep it in place with my foot, but it only covered half of the leak. Pretty soon the boat got so filled up I could hardly pull it at all, but I kept those oars working like they were the blades of a propeller.

Someway we made it to the shore at a little dock in front of where the Hindus and the Arabs lived, just as the boat was going down. I got the boat up on the dock and looked at the bottom. There was a big hole where two of the boards had been spread apart, like it'd hit on a rock. And I knew, like the emptying of the tank that hole wasn't a accident.

A night or so after that we were listening to the radio before going to bed when I saw Aziza look kind of funny and hurry out to the kitchen.

She came back in a minute. "I thought I heard someone, Yance," she said.

I hadn't heard a sound and I thought she'd made a mistake. But next afternoon I was in the store moving some cans of corn beef, when all of a sudden I felt a awful pain in my stomach that pretty near doubled me over. I tried not to pay any attention to it, and finished moving the cans and started opening up some crates of hardware. But the pain got worse and worse.

I finally put away the hatchet I was using and sat down in a chair. "I got to stop," I said to Louie. "I hope I ain't got blackwater fever again."

Louie got pretty scared, I guess, and he called Aziza and they got me into bed. I had a pretty bad time laying there all afternoon. This time I thought I was really going to die.

And then about dark the launch come up the river, and lucky for me a doctor from one of the mines was one of the passengers, and he took one look at me and he said right away I'd been poisoned.

He gave me all kinds of medicine, and Aziza nursed me wonderful again with Miss Peckham helping, too, and I pulled through all right. But course I knew who gave me that poison.

CHAPTER NINETEEN

As soon as I was feeling a little better Louie wanted me
to send word about what had happened to the police.

But I wouldn't do it. I couldn't prove anything, and
even if I could, the way I heard the Englishmen that rode
the launch saying, if you ever got the police coming

229

around these African people, that was the end of you sure.

I guess it was a couple of weeks after Louie talked to me and I was still pretty shaky, when I see the launch of the District Commissioner stop at the dock, and the two black soldiers come out with the Commissioner. They all marched down to the store, and the Commissioner come in and I shook his hand. But it was like when I put my hand down a bucket of dry ice in a drugstore in San Antonio.

He didn't take a drink of Scotch this time, and he didn't even sit down, just stood there near the door. I could see he was pretty mad.

"I regret I must take up this matter, my dear Cullum, when you are still so obviously unwell," he said. "But it is my duty as an officer of the Crown. I have no desire to send you back to your country in a coffin. It would cost your government and mine much embarrassment and some money."

He smoothed his little mustache. "I have already told you we have a most delicate situation here. I understand your feelings about the young chief's wives and I may say I am in sympathy. But any changes in the customs of the African population are matters of the most careful adjustment, which must be worked out largely by themselves. I implore you, do not interfere in this matter of the women any further. Otherwise you will bring about a disaster that may go even beyond the borders of this colony. And I ask you to please so counsel Miss Peckham."

He kind of softened a little. "If I may give you a personal word of advice. From a cynical old civil servant who has been long in Africa. Try to make friends with this chief's son. He is a weak young man, very susceptible to flattery. Flatter him. And give him presents whenever you can."

A week later Suleiman came, too, looking worried, his big stomach bouncing like a balloon. He went around with me, and saw the patch I'd put in the gasboat, and he said the same as the Commissioner.

"This is bad, Yance," he told me. "The black women are getting excited in the villages all along the river. Even my own wives are talking. Please be careful, Yance."

Well, like you can see, I ain't one of those fellows that have to be told something twice. I explained to Miss Peckham how it was, and she was awful sorry, but we stopped the women from coming to the Club. Bathsheeba and the other black wives raised a terrible fuss. But there wasn't anything different I could do. And after a little while it looked like things were going to be all right, the way they were before.

About this time Miss Peckham got a letter from her sister in Liberia asking her not to stay in Yembasi any longer. They were making the mission in Liberia bigger and needed her bad, so she decided she'd have to go.

That gasboat sinking and the poisoning had got me worried something might happen to Aziza, and I thought maybe I ought to send her off with Miss Peckham for a while.

But when I told her she laughed like the bells again. "Nothing can happen to me, Yance," she said. She touched a little black leather square had dots on it like a dice that she wore around her neck. "I have this charm my mother's mother gave me. She was ninety years old when she died, and she said that with this charm I will live even longer."

A few days later Miss Peckham went around to all the black women and their babies and told them good-by, and me and Louie went with her in the launch to a village near the mines where they had the airport now. And the plane came in, and Miss Peckham looked at Louie, and her eyes filled with tears.

She gave him a little Bible with his name on it in gold. "It is from the members of the Adult Sunday School in Fall River," she said. "The same class to which you belong in Bab-El-Kebir. I am going now to where there will be many converts. And I will study the way these simple black men are brought to our Saviour. When I have learned, I will return to Bab-El-Kebir and finish my work there and have many among the Arabs also who have come to our Lord."

She straightened a crease in her stiff black dress. "And when the benches in the Sunday School are crowded with smiling Arab children, it will be you, my dear son Mohammed, who will teach them the good life. And each third Sunday in May I will put flowers on the table and remember our precious anniversary. For though I have as many accepting our Lord as there were cedars in Lebanon, you will be the pearl in my crown. . . . God keep you both."

And she climbed into the plane and was gone.

We caught the launch going back to the store. There were some English people going down the river and they were awful nice and friendly. But Louie and me didn't say very much. Someway we didn't feel like talking.

Things were awful quiet after that for a while. I did

the way the Commissioner said and tried to kind of make up with the chief's son, though I didn't like him any better than before.

And then Suleiman got a lot of bicycles—I guess they were surplus but I ain't sure—and he sent some up to me. They were good bicycles, and I picked out the prettiest, all painted green and gold, and hung some strings of fancy beads over the handle bars, and sent Gwani over with it to the chief's son.

Gwani came back in a little while, and the chief's son wasn't ten minutes behind and I never seen him so happy.

He talked to Gwani a minute, all smiles, and then put out his hand to me.

"He says you and he are brothers now, Master," Gwani told me. "He says you and he will not quarrel any more."

He rode that bicycle everywhere, proud as a bantam rooster. And he'd smile and wave at me whenever I come within half a mile. The other bicycles sold fast but his was the best, and when he started racing with the other black fellows and they always let him win, this time I didn't say a word.

Some more bicycles came and I sold them in the villages around. Everywhere you went along the river you could see the black fellows riding with voodoo charms and little idols tied behind the seats. They liked the bicycles almost as much as they did the baseball.

One queer thing, you couldn't leave the bicycles out in the jungle for even a few hours or they'd be gone. The big chimpanzees hated them, I don't know why. If they ever found one out in the woods with nobody around, they'd make terrible faces and scream the way monkeys do, and tear the wheels and everything apart until it was nothing but a pile of rubber and wire. The black people lost a couple of bicycles that way.

Everything was going nice again. I had the Club running good, even though Miss Peckham was gone. We got a Bingo game in the surplus that should have been sent like the baseball games to some canteen or PX, I guess. And I remembered how lodges and churches and everybody back in the States were always having Bingo for something, so I thought it'd be a good thing to start the game in the Club. Louie and me stayed up front reading off the numbers and the black people sure liked it. They'd have sat around every night playing until sunup if Louie and me hadn't stopped to get some sleep.

The store kept doing fine. And then I heard that the power plant I'd bought was on its way at last and right after that it came. It was a good plant, but I had a kind of disappointment. It was low voltage, about sixty volts, and the laundry machinery was a hundred and twenty. I'd just plain forgot to ask about that.

Soon as I could get a transformer it'd be all right, but the transformer'd take a couple of months, and I didn't want to wait that long to use the electricity. Suleiman wrote he was anxious to have lights and things in the store, too, because he knew it'd boost business. Course he said he'd pay me for the current. So I decided I'd go ahead with the wiring and we could use the electricity right away.

I figured I'd put up a new little building right next to the store where I'd keep the power plant and have the laundry. And while we were at it, I'd leave room to open a couple of new departments. There were a lot of launches on the river now making trips to the mines, and I'd been figuring it'd be a good idea to start selling parts for motor boats, and maybe radios and batteries and things, too. When you got electricity you can do plenty.

Suleiman had said any time I wanted to start my own little place it'd be all right, as long as I didn't sell anything that what they call competed with him. And I knew he was figuring on making me a partner, anyway. He hadn't said much about it lately, but I knew it was just because we hadn't had a chance to do a lot of talking.

Mr. Ziegler came by about that time, and I ordered a lot of stock for the new store, and signed another paper he gave me, and the stock came right away. And I put it in one of the little warehouses we had down by the dock, and started the new building.

I had it pretty near finished, and was working on the wiring and the power plant, when the English fellow that ran the launch got to talking to me. He said it was getting on toward May 24, that was what they called the Queen's Birthday, and he figured it'd be nice to start the electricity then.

He said he'd heard a big fellow from London making a speech to the black men saying how England and the Queen had brought light to the people in Africa. And he figured electricity'd be the same way.

He told me the English celebrated the Queen's Birthday like we do the Fourth of July. I didn't remind him that the Fourth was when we beat the English, just the same as I didn't say anything the time I met that Lord when I was in the camp in London—ain't no use hurting people's feelings—and he said they had fireworks and parades and field meets just like us.

I thought that about the electricity and the Birthday

was a fine idea. And I knew the District Commissioner would sure like me doing something about the Queen that way. So I started planning things right off. The baseball and the bicycles were still going strong, so I figured I'd get some teams from the other villages to have some ball games and bicycle races, and maybe a little bow-and-arrow shooting and other things the black people'd like.

Pretty soon it was the day before the Birthday, and I put some of the radios and batteries into the new store and it looked real nice. And I checked the wires and the bulbs everywhere, and they were working good. I'd put a lot of bulbs inside the store and plenty of them outside, too, along the dock and the little warehouses and even the hamburger stand, so the people passing on the river could see them after dark. I knew the place'd really shine.

Everybody was happy because they knew the holiday was tomorrow. The black fellows from the other villages that were going to be in the baseball games and the other contests started coming that afternoon in their canoes, so they'd be sure not to miss anything, and they all were laughing and having a fine time.

The village looked real pretty. I had it all decorated with English flags and some pictures of the Queen. And then on the store I had a American flag to show I was a American. And I put one on the hamburger stand, too.

It sure made me think of Black Spring on the Fourth of July. It'd have been nice if I could have had the American flag a cowboy lived in Black Spring that was too old to work used to put in front of his house every Fourth. It was pretty near as big as a freight car and he'd made it all out of the tops off pop bottles.

Next morning after the sun come up I set off some

236

bombs I'd made out of dynamite that was going up to the mines. I'd have liked to have some real fireworks the way we had for the Wheel but I couldn't get any in time. And then about nine o'clock I come out of the store with Aziza and we walked over to the open place in front of the clubhouse.

Aziza was wearing a American flag like me, and had a red, white, and blue ribbon in her hair. I'd have liked her to be all dressed up in the American flag the way they had a girl do every night at the end of the rodeo, but I thought since this was for England maybe it wouldn't be right.

First there were to be some drum contests, playing them big African drums, and Aziza hit a drum with a stick to start things going, the way the President throws a ball to open the first ball game. And then there was some dancing, men wearing awful-looking masks like the devil-faces kids have on Halloween, and then men dressed in lion skins and other men hunting them with bows and arrows.

And then the baseball games began. Some of the fellows were wearing animal tails and it was sure funny to watch the tails flying when a man run around the bases or chased a fly ball. We had a couple of games going at once because there was so many teams, and that way I wasn't watching close. But pretty soon in the game where the Yembasi fellows were playing another village, I saw they were all getting awful mad.

I asked Gwani what was the matter.

"They are angry at each other, Master," he said. "Before the English came the people of Yembasi and the other black men would come in the night and attack each others' villages. And they who were the victors would take their enemies' women as slaves and kill all the men and the children. They are thinking of those days now, Master."

Well, pretty soon they were punching each other. And a couple of times fellows swung a bat. And I looked and saw the other teams were fighting the same way. And all the time, between innings, they'd rush off into the trees and drink palm wine their friends had brought, and I began getting worried.

To make it worse the Yembasi team lost the first game, and then they started losing the second, too. And pretty soon bats were whirling everywhere. I stopped all the games so there wouldn't be a real battle.

By then it was time to eat and take a rest while the sun was hottest. That African sun beating down on you was like putting your head inside a red-hot stove. But instead of resting all they did was drink more palm wine, and everybody got madder.

Louie was getting awful nervous. "It's bad, Joe," he said. "I wish we were back in Bab-El-Kebir with the Ouleds."

We got things going after lunch but no matter what they tried to do the Yembasi people always got beat. And then the chief's son came into it and things went bad fast.

I guess it'd been the same even if he hadn't been there, the way everybody was feeling. He hadn't done anything before, just stood watching kind of sarcastic. But now we began the bicycle races, and he came up riding the bike I gave him, cocky as a bantam rooster again.

I knew it meant trouble, because he was a terrible rider and today it wasn't like when he was with the Yembasi people. He didn't mean nothing to the black fellows from the other villages.

He started in the race and got 'way behind in a minute. And he tried to go fast and fell flat on the ground. He got up and climbed on the seat again, and rode kind of slow to where all the people were watching, because now the race was over. And I thought he was going to be all right.

And then I saw him hop off the seat and throw the bicycle down and jump on it with both feet like a wild man. And he picked up a big club laying there and beat the bike to pieces.

I was really worried now and I made Louie take Aziza back to the store.

The next thing was the bow-and-arrow shooting. And I saw the chief's son talking to his father and drinking palm wine by the gallon. I hoped the son had drunk too much to try the shooting. But pretty soon he come walking over, with his face all swollen from the liquor and carrying a bow and some arrows.

All the other black fellows had been hitting the bull's eye in the target I'd made. They were wonderful shots. Better than a Indian. But he shoots and shoots and didn't get nowhere near. The last time he didn't even hit the target.

And then all of a sudden he began to yell and started popping arrows at the black men that come from the other villages. And the other fellows shot back, and in a minute arrows were flying thick as bees when you've upset a hive.

I saw some of the Yembasi men laying on the ground looked like they were hurt bad. And then I saw the fellows from the other villages running down to the docks with a big bunch of Yembasi people after them. The strangers jumped into their canoes and paddled up the river. And the Yembasi men run along the bank and kept shooting arrows till they're out of sight.

I went back to look at the ones laying on the ground. I wanted to help them and bring them over to the store. But the old chief and the chief's son wouldn't let me touch them. I could see the old man had been drinking heavy, too. I never seen him that way before. And some of the black men picked up the fellows on the ground and carried them off. And they looked like they're dead.

Gwani watched them go and got more mournful-looking than ever.

"They say you have brought disgrace to the people of Yembasi, Master," he told me. "They have drunk too much palm wine. I think you had better go back to the store and take your gun, Master."

I did what he said and walked back to the trading post. And pretty soon I heard the tom-toms going in the village with a kind of funny beat and I knew things were getting dangerous. I put Aziza in a back room where she wouldn't get hurt if a arrow came through the window. And me and Louie and Gwani took our guns and waited.

After a while it got dark, and I thought maybe it'd kind of calm them down if I turned on the electric lights. So I clicked the switches, and when the lights came on it was so bright it was like a explosion. You could see the palm trees in front of the store and the jungle across the river plain as day. You could even see a big horse antelope down at the water drinking. He stood there staring, kind of blinded for a minute, and then he ran away.

After I put the lights on it got quiet for a little while. But pretty soon the tom-toms started beating again. I figured I'd better leave the lights on anyway so we could see what was going on.

The tom-toms kept on getting louder and pretty soon the black people come out from the village and began dancing in a open place back of the palm trees.

They weren't wearing the uniforms and dungarees now. They were all pretty near naked and some had their faces all painted with stripes or had big red or yellow eyes painted on their bodies and their foreheads. And some of them had masks and strings of crocodile teeth and little animal skulls.

The dancers took spears and clubs after a while and begun shaking them at the store like the first night we come and they were having the funeral for the fellow that died. Only this time it wasn't for a black man. The way they were acting you could see this funeral was going to be for us.

I jumped when I heard a noise at the back of the store and swung around fast with my rifle. But then I heard a bracelet clink and I knew it was Aziza.

She spoke soft and quiet the way she always did when things weren't going right.

"I wish to stay with you, Yance," she said.

And she moved up by me where I was watching at the window.

The dancing got wilder and wilder. The men started a fire now and I tell you it wasn't nice to see those big red and yellow eyes on their foreheads bouncing up and down in front of the flames like the eyes of some terrible animals. And then some fellows came up all painted white, and they began dancing, too. And they looked like ghosts.

The flames got bigger, and pretty soon I saw little points of fire going around, and in a minute all the black men were carrying torches. And I knew it was to burn down the store.

I took my rifle and started toward the door.

"I'm going out there and try to talk to them," I said to Gwani. "I seen plenty of those fellows pretty near every day coming in to buy something. There ain't hardly one of them that I haven't give some candy or tobacco to. They'll sure listen to me."

Gwani shook his head. "You can do nothing, Master. They will strike you with a spear the way they kill a deer or a hyena. They are drunk with the palm wine, Master."

They danced with the torches for a minute, and then they began chanting some queer song that made your blood run cold. And then all of a sudden they swung off and went up the river.

I couldn't figure it out for a minute, and then I saw they were going toward the edge of the village where the traders lived. Pretty soon I saw a red glow in the sky that got bigger and bigger, and showers of sparks flew up like the night I saw a lumber yard burn up in San Antonio.

"They are burning the houses of the Arabs and Hindus," said Gwani. "After that they will come here."

CHAPTER TWENTY

THE FLAMES WERE STILL ROARING when I saw the torches moving toward us again and the chanting got louder. And then I could see the big eyes and the fellows like ghosts coming down the bank, jumping like they're crazy.

They stopped in front of one of our little warehouses, and in a second somebody threw a torch and the building was blazing. I couldn't see that happen without doing something, so I told Gwani to grab his gun and I took mine, too. And we left Louie to look after Aziza, and ran outside to try to stop the fire.

The black fellows moved off a little way when they saw our guns and stood a minute, kind of undecided. And then they backed toward the tall grass growing there, and quick as a fox they were gone.

Gwani and me went up to the warehouse and tried to beat out the flames, but it wasn't any use. The thatch they were made of burned too fast, and in no time the building and everything in it was finished.

I looked off toward where the black fellows had gone, hoping I could see the chief maybe, and talk to him. But there wasn't a soul, only a high wall of grass, all lit up by the fire and the electric lights along the river.

I called out, but there wasn't any answer. There was just the echo of my own voice and the frogs croaking like you were shooting a pistol.

I walked right up to the edge of the grass this time and called out again. I was sure if I could find the chief we'd be all right. Gwani was walking a little way off, crouched like a leopard and watching the ground in front of him every second.

And then, I don't know why, I guess because I got used to things that way when I was a cowboy, I felt something coming and ducked, just as a black fellow big as a elephant jumped out of some low bushes you wouldn't think'd hide a rabbit and swung at me with a war club. Because I ducked it didn't hit me square on top of the head. If it had it'd have broke my skull like a eggshell. But it kind of glanced along one side back of my ear instead. I went down like the last pin in a bowling alley. It was a terrible blow and pretty near broke my shoulder blade, too.

I lay on the ground awful numb, not able to move for a minute, and then I saw this giant fellow swing the club high in the air to finish me off this time. I thought I was done for, because I couldn't even raise a finger, when I see Gwani that'd run over jump on him like a leopard sure enough, and take the club away, and give him a good whack that laid him out like a stone. And then he pulled me to my feet and helped me run back toward the store.

I couldn't go fast, feeling like my knees were caving under me every step, and I guess we made a fine target. I was just going through the door when Gwani jerked me down quick, and there was a funny whirring sound, and something hit the wood just above me. It dropped to the ground, and even numb as I was I could see it was a throwing knife with eight blades like razors. If it'd hit anywhere it would have cut through me the way a butcher does a sausage.

Another knife came after it, and then a whole bunch of arrows, but by this time I was inside again.

I held onto the window sill so I wouldn't fall. "Get me a little water somebody, will you?" I said.

But even before I'd said it, Aziza had gone for a wash basin. And she bathed my face and tied up the cut that ran all down the side of my head. I felt like I'd been run over by a steam roller. The water helped and pretty soon I could think a little better. Though I sure wasn't in any shape to keep off a army of wild black people.

Things were quiet for a little while. And then I saw the torches moving forward and the flames started up again. This time it was another little storehouse that had most of the radios and batteries I'd bought from Mr. Ziegler. But I knew there wasn't any use trying to go out there any more. We'd just have to stay and watch it burn. All we could do now was to try to save the store and our lives.

The warehouse went up all of a sudden, like a little

volcano, and burned to a cinder. And then the black people set fire to the dockhouse and the hamburger stand. I hated to see the stand go. Those pictures of Africa Aziza and me had painted on it, the trees and the lions and the monkeys, were sure pretty.

The dockhouse burned slower than the others, because it was kind of wet, I guess, and being right there by the river you could see it again in the water. And then all of a sudden the electric lights in the store and everywhere went out. I guess the fire had shorted the wires somewhere.

For a minute it was terrible dark, but there was enough light from the flames and the starlight to make out things around us. And pretty soon I could see maybe twenty of the black fellows that had the big eyes painted on them slide out from the grass like spotted snakes, and come crawling in a kind of half-moon toward the store. And they were all carrying spears or big knives.

Maybe they'd been scared of the electricity before, and now the lights were out they weren't afraid any more.

They stopped a little way off, like they were waiting for something, and then the tom-toms back in the grass started going like they'd burst your ears. And a minute later a torch went flying to the little building near the store where we put the people from the launch when they stayed overnight.

I started to run out to save it, because I figured that was really part of the store, but Gwani and Louie pulled me back. I guess that being hit on the head had made me a little bit crazy. I wouldn't have lasted a second if I'd have gone out that door.

The torch caught now and the place went up like another volcano. Smoke came in all around us, the building was so near. The fumes were so bad we were coughing and choking all the time. We could hardly breathe.

The fellows in the half-moon started crawling toward us again, and with their black skins on the ground that way all you could see was the knives they were holding and the big yellow eyes coming closer and closer.

And then a second half-moon came behind them, and these were the fellows painted white like ghosts. But funny thing, they didn't throw a torch at the store. I figured they wanted to catch us alive, and then when they were ready they'd kill us some terrible way.

A lot of arrows came through the windows, ripping the screens like they were tissue paper. And then a whole mob of the black fellows came out of the grass far back, so many they looked like those big African black ants, collecting around some little animal they were going to drag off to their anthill.

Louie and Gwani were each at a window with their guns, and I stood at the door by Aziza, holding my gun, too. We watched the circles of the men with the eyes and the ghost men get narrower and narrower, and waited awful quiet, the way you did in the war when a bunch of Germans were coming and you knew it was them or you.

And then all of a sudden I heard some kind of wild war whoops off in the trees. And the tom-toms stopped like somebody'd punched a hole in them. And then a lot of black men painted like rainbows and wearing a fancy kind of animal tails and carrying knives shaped like grass hooks came running up, screaming like wildcats. And the fellows with the painted eyes and the ghost men that were closing in on us jumped up and turned around, and began fighting like tigers with the rainbow men that had the tails. And all you could hear was clubs thwacking and men falling to the ground like when you're cutting trees.

And pretty soon I could see the ghosts and the fellows with the painted eyes run off toward the river, and back of them came the fellows with the tails, swinging their grass-hook knives and shooting arrows and yelling worse than Indians when they were raiding a covered-wagon camp out West.

And then things got quiet as a graveyard and you couldn't hear a sound except the frogs croaking again, or every once in a while a timber on one of the burned buildings caving in, sending up sparks like the fireworks I'd wanted for the Queen's Birthday.

We didn't find out what happened till after daylight when a old woman that took care of Aziza come over to the store. The men from the next village had got wild after the Yembasi people chased them that afternoon, so they come back that night to get even. They ran the Yembasi fellows 'way off so they'd know they'd had a good licking, and then they all went home.

Aziza cooked us breakfast. I guess we didn't eat very much. And then after I was sure everything had quieted down and the trouble was over we went around to see what the fire had done. There wasn't anything left of the little building where the people stayed and the warehouses and the other things but a pile of red coals and ashes. And some of the Hindu and Arab houses at the edge of town were the same way.

The launch come by around noon and the mine doctor was on it and sewed up the big cut in my head. He told me I was sure a lucky man. Like I said, if it had been a few inches farther up, my head would have been broke like a burglar smashes a glass window.

The black people started coming back next day one by one, looking kind of ashamed of themselves. And then the old chief come in, too, and he didn't say anything, but I could tell he was awful sorry. He'd have never let them act that way if he hadn't drunk all that palm wine. And then everybody that had been hurt come, too, and there wasn't any doctor around so I fixed them up with the medicines I had at the store the best I could.

I didn't see the chief's son anywhere or the big fellow that hit me with the club, and the black people told me they'd gone away for a while.

Course I felt terrible about all Suleiman's things and mine that got burned up. But you can't let trouble stop you. Every time in the States a town burns in a big fire or is wiped out by a tornado, you read in the paper how the people start building a new town right away. And I figured that's what we had to do here in Yembasi.

Lucky, the laundry machinery wasn't touched, because it was in the new building next to the store, so that when the transformer came along I could get it started quick, and I could get the new departments going, selling the radios and the parts for motor boats because lucky for me, too, I had put a lot of those in the new building. Then later maybe I could put in a gas pump and boat repair business. And course I could get a new hamburger stand made in a couple of days.

I guess maybe it was a week later and I was in the store looking over boat catalogs, figuring what I'm going to do, when I see the District Commissioner's launch come up

249

to the burned dockhouse. The black men were out in the woods now, cutting a lot of logs so we could make it and the other buildings better than ever. And the District Commissioner come out, and I was surprised when I seen that Suleiman's there, too.

They didn't come to the store right away, just went around everywhere looking over the damage. And I knew that was a bad sign. And then they come in, and the Commissioner's face was kind of white and Suleiman's stomach didn't bounce hardly at all.

The Commissioner didn't even shake hands with me this time. He just stood there looking so cold he could freeze meat.

"This is most deplorable, Mr. Cullum," he said. "You have caused a riot which might have spread far beyond this village if it had not been for the prompt action of our officers elsewhere. You have caused bodily harm to come to a number of Africans under his Majesty's protection. You have caused the destruction by arson of the property of half a dozen Hindu and Arab families. To say nothing of the loss occasioned to Mr. Suleiman and yourself and your own personal injury. I have been in touch with the Consul of your country at Accra. I must inform you, Mr. Cullum, that both he and I and both our governments are greatly concerned."

He kept talking that way for a while, and then Suleiman said the same thing, and I felt terrible, though looking back I couldn't see a thing I'd done wrong.

It was like one time when I was cabbing in San Antonio and there was a accident with two cars right ahead of me, and I come to court as a witness, and the Judge gave me a awful lecture on bad driving, even though I didn't have a thing to do with what happened.

They kept on and I got to feeling worse and worse. And then I got to thinking about it and all of a sudden I got kind of fed up.

"I tell you, if I had the money I'd sure buy tickets for Aziza and me back to the States," I said. "But after the fire I ain't got a nickel, besides all the money I owe Mr. Ziegler for the stock and the power plant."

Well, there's plenty of fellows I know that say people ain't nice. But after what happened that day, it's sure not the way I figure. The minute I said that about owing the money, Suleiman jumped up, all smiles.

"You needn't worry about the money you owe, Yance," he said. "To let you go back to your own country I will gladly pay Mr. Ziegler myself."

And the District Commissioner acted just the same. All the other English people said he was awful stuffy, and before then it always looked that way to me. But now he was all smiles like Suleiman.

"You need not trouble a moment about your fare, Mr. Cullum," he said. "My government will gladly pay the money necessary to get you back to your home. If necessary, I will take it out of my own personal funds."

He thought a minute. "The mail boat leaves from Takoradi for New York on the twelfth. If we start early in the morning I will take you down to Imboku, where we can catch the train to Takoradi and arrive there in ample time."

Aziza and me rushed around like a couple of prairie dogs getting things packed up. We were all ready to leave when it come to me that I'd forgot all about the laundry machinery, and I sure didn't want to lose that. But Suleiman said not to worry, that when I got settled and knew what I wanted to do he'd send it anywhere. And me and Aziza shook hands with him, and went down with Louie to the wharf.

Louie begged the Commissioner to let him come with us to Imboku, and he sat with us all the way going down the river.

We got to Imboku and went over with the Commissioner to the police station, a pretty little place with a fine flower garden. The Commissioner sent off some telegrams and then we went over to the little railroad depot. And the porters carried my bags onto the funny train that was waiting there, though it wouldn't be leaving for a couple of hours.

Louie told me to pay each of the porters a shilling, that's fifteen cents, and I started to give them the money when I seen his face change quick, and he pulled back my hand.

"No. No, Joe," he said. "Give them only three pence, a fourth of a shilling. This is the regular price. I arranged with them to divide the nine pence extra. But it would not be right to cheat you when you are going away."

We waited around the depot and Louie went off for a while. He came back just before the train was getting ready to start, carrying a beautiful bouquet of flowers, and gave them to Aziza.

She thanked him and they were so pretty she asked where they came from.

He looked kind of proud. "I stole them from the police station," he said.

Just then the train whistled, and he kissed me on both cheeks the way the Arabs and the French do, and we climbed onto the passenger car at the end.

The train started moving. He stood on the station platform, smiling and waving under his red hat, just like the organ-grinder had trained his monkey to do when kids came around. And then the train swung into some trees, and I didn't see him any more.

And I knew I'd lost my best friend.

Well, I'd never have thought it, but that District Commissioner turned out to be the finest fellow you ever saw. I figured he'd sure leave us at Imboku. But he didn't. He came right on the train with us. There'd been some bad storms, and the track was washed out in a couple of places and it held us up for a while. And I never seen a man so nervous, talking to the train crew, and finding out if they could make up the time so we'd catch the boat. He rode all the way to Takoradi.

Like he thought, the train was almost half a day behind getting in, and I was sure we were too late. But we got out at the station, and the American Consul was there, a young fellow in a helmet, just as nice as the Commissioner. And they rushed us down to the dock in a big, fancy car. And sure enough the boat was still there, with the people on her pacing up and down, kind of mad because they weren't leaving.

The Commissioner said they'd arranged to hold the boat for me. Both him and the American Consul didn't want me to miss it for anything.

They were sure nice.

The boat started right out, and we had a fine trip. We come here to New York and we been here ever since.

New York's a nice town. They give you good franks. But the hamburgers ain't as good as Texas.

I worked in the Ford plant in Jersey for a while to get some money. I got a job in the Parts Department. And about a month ago I met a Arab that owned a little Arab pastry shop over on Washington Street where some of the Arabs live, and he said he'd sell me the place cheap so I bought it.

It's a good little business and we're doing all right. Like I said, Aziza's a fine cook and she can make wonderful pastry. I been wanting Ma to taste some of it, but Aziza ain't met her yet. Ma's been wanting to come on but she's been kind of busy with Mr. Bradley down in Houston and she ain't been able to get away.

Course the pastry business ain't but for a little while. Soon as I get some money saved up we're going back to Africa and start the laundry again. In Johannesburg like we figured. Or maybe down at Leopoldville in the Belgian Congo. You can't beat having a laundry.

Last few days I been looking at some new kind of laundry machinery they're making now that I figure I'll take with me. Funny thing, in the place where I was looking yesterday I met a fellow come from Dallas, and a couple of weeks ago in a restaurant I met a fellow from San Antonio.

But I ain't met anybody yet from Black Spring.

ABOUT THE AUTHOR

BEN LUCIEN BURMAN, who was born in the river town of Covington, Kentucky, has been called America's greatest living interpreter. He is famous for his novels of the Mississippi. His *Steamboat Round the Bend,* which became Will Rogers's most successful film, and *Blow for a Landing* have become American classics.

Mr. Burman wrote his first story on a toy typewriter when he was seven years old and has been writing ever since. He was wounded during World War I at Soissons, and his writing was interrupted for a while, but after the war he became a reporter for the Boston *Herald,* and later the old New York *World.* When Ben Burman was twenty-six, he gave up newspaper work to concentrate on fiction.

The author, with his wife, Alice Caddy, who illustrates his books, lived for several years in North and Central Africa, where they collected the material for *The Street of the Laughing Camel.*

Mr. Burman's books have been translated into many languages and he has been decorated by the French government with the Legion of Honor. He is frequently referred to as the modern Mark Twain both in literature and on the lecture platform.